Eliza: A Story of Overcoming Limitations

Women of God: Book 2

Deanna L. Stalnaker

E-book: ISBN # 978-0-9894267-1-8
ISBN-13: 9780989426749
ISBN-10: 0989426742

www.kardeesangelpublishing.com

Library of Congress Control Number: 2013921268
KarDee's Angel Publishing, Tobaccoville, NC

Other Books and Facebook pages by Author:

Tea Time with Jesus

Kardee's Angels

Dedication

First and foremost I want to thank God for giving me the inspiration to write this story. Without His direction this would be a book devoid of meaning and it would only be an exercise of putting words on paper.

Next I would like to dedicate this book to all of those who through some unforeseen tragedy, illness, or by birth have to deal with living through their extreme disabilities. God be with each of you.

Lastly, I want to thank my family and friends for all your support. You've been great!

Acknowledgments:

All scriptures quoted are from the
King James Version of the Bible

I would like to thank the organization of *Joni and Friends* for allowing me to refer to their organization in my story. Their website is listed at the end of the book in the 'Afterword' section. It is a Christian organization for people with handicaps around the world.

Disclaimer:

Clairmonte, NC, is a fictional town and the characters, events, and places in this novel are not based on any persons, either living or dead, and the events and facilities are also fictitious. They are totally my creation. Any similarities between these characters, events, and facilities are purely coincidental.

Table of Contents

Prologue

I can do all things through Christ who strengtheneth me.
Philippians 4:13

I would come to appreciate that verse from the Bible. It has become my mantra over the last few years. Every day I would have to reaffirm my faith to keep me from becoming totally destitute from my affliction.

Three years ago I was riding in a car with my two friends, Zoe and Billie. We were returning home from a visit with our friend, Jobella. We were to be her bridesmaids in her wedding and that particular Saturday we were having a planning party.

We decided to leave a little early. Jobella was getting a little too 'preachy' with us and we were all getting a little uncomfortable with that. Jobella was always talking about how great God was, even after everything she went through this past year. All of us had been good friends when we were growing up, but I don't think that she realized we had our own lives to live, and we didn't want her preaching to us.

So we made our excuses and left in a hurry after her talk. Since the three of us were riding together we had to leave at the same time. Zoe was driving, and Billie was sitting in the front seat with her, and I was in the back poking my head between them to keep up with their conversation. I wasn't wearing my seat belt so I could be closer to them. That was not a smart thing to do, especially in that horrible rainstorm. If I had been wearing it, I might not be in the shape I'm in today.

I did have a life before that horrific accident that day. I was very athletic, and I had participated in a lot of sports, especially in high school. I grew up in an upper middle class neighborhood close to my three closest friends. We hung out after school, and for the most part we got along great. We went to the same church and with the exception of Jobella, the rest of us often got into trouble partying every Friday night and then repented every Sunday in church. This went on for a couple of years until the three of us gave up on going to church. We were having too much fun, and going to church made us feel guilty. Our families quit going shortly after we dropped out. It's almost as if the only reason they went was because of us. Jobella was the only one who stayed faithful in the church along with the rest of her family.

Even with our differences, Jobella and I planned on going to Duke University in the fall and we were going to be roommates that first year when all her problems began. She was going into law and I was going to be majoring in whatever else I could find that wouldn't be too hard to get good grades in. Needless to say, I had to start school without her my freshman year.

I was going to miss having her as a roommate at Duke again this year, as well, since she would be living in this apartment with her husband, Steven.

I was lucky in that I would be getting a scholarship in sports that would pay most of my tuition. I was an avid runner, and had won several regional track meets as I was growing up. I would've been starting my sophomore year at Duke in four weeks when it happened…

Chapter 1

Zoe called me on her cell phone. "Eliza, are you about ready to go to Jobella's apartment yet? We'll be over in about fifteen minutes to pick you up."

"Sure, no problem. I'll be ready when you get here. Can't wait!"

We were getting ready to go to our friend's house to help her plan her wedding, and have a "tea" party. It sounded like it would be a lot of fun, and it would be great seeing each other again. It had been over a year since Jobella had lost both of her parents in a house fire and her brother and sister were put in foster care. If that wasn't enough, two weeks later, she suffered the brutal rape by her uncle and her boyfriend almost died after he was beat up in the same attack. She spent the next six months in the hospital on the mental unit while her boyfriend was in a coma and then he was in rehab for the past six months. We all looked forward to her getting married and settling down now, and hopefully, getting her brother and sister back soon after the wedding.

We were good friends again now, but each of the three of us had a falling out with her after we tried to 'preach' to her while she was in the mental ward at the hospital.

While I was getting dressed, I thought back to my visit with her while she was in the hospital. I tried to talk with her about God, but she didn't take it too well. She was depressed and angry over what happened to her and her family, and she just wouldn't listen to anyone, including me, her best friend. It was hard seeing her wallowing in self-pity. I tried to tell her that I thought God wasn't happy with her for some reason and was punishing her. There had to be a reason she was going through all those tragic things. In hindsight, that was really a dumb thing to say on my part, because if anyone was close to being perfect, it was Jobella. Thinking back now, I can understand why she was so mad at me. If God were a vengeful God, I should've been the one going through those trials, not her. I'm the one who disobeyed my parent's, and lied about spending the night with my boyfriend, and asked Jobella to cover for me. I was always getting into trouble, and she was always there to bail me out.

Billie, Zoe, and I would often go to parties where there would be drinking and drugs and guys. We couldn't stay away from all the evils we heard about every Sunday morning. All three of us finally stopped going to church after a while. We knew we were hypocrites, so we all decided that we could hide from God by not going to church and we often lied to our parents and made up excuses why we couldn't go. Our parents grew tired of the whole church thing as well, so they didn't mind it when we didn't want to go anymore. Jobella is the only one of us that continued to go to church with her family and get anything out of it. Looking back, I don't know why she even still considered us her friends. We just didn't have too much in common anymore after leaving church.

While we were upset over what our friend had to endure over the past year, we kind of gloated, in a way, because here she was so good and look what God had done to her, while the three of us were always acting badly, and God didn't punish us at all. I think we all were looking for answers about the proverbial question of 'Why do bad things happen to good people?'.

"Hi, guys." I called out, as they were pulling into my driveway. We decided to all ride together because it was about a thirty-minute drive to Jobella's apartment. Gas prices were getting out of control, so we decided to car pool. Zoe had a new silver colored SUV. She had the largest vehicle of the three of us, so we decided to ride with her and share the expenses.

"Are you all excited to be in Jobella's wedding?" I asked as I was getting into her car.

"It should be fun. This is the first time I've ever been a bridesmaid," stated Zoe. "I wonder what she has planned."

"This must be tough for her, trying to plan her wedding without her mom and dad. I would hate it if I had to get married without my parents being there," Billie added.

"I understand her lawyer friend is going to help her. She's even going to be her matron of honor," I replied. "I think she said that Steven's parents were helping her plan everything as well."

We talked back and forth the rest of the way to her apartment, catching up on all the latest gossip and what our plans were for the fall. Billie said that she was going back to the local community college to be a medical assistant. She just had one year left. She also said she was planning on getting married on Valentine's Day the next year. Zoe was getting ready to go art school in New York. She wanted to be a fashion designer. She's always been the 'artsy' one of us. As for me, I had been in summer school and had a new boyfriend that I'd been dating for a month now.

By the time we finished updating each other with information about ourselves, we were at Jobella's. We made excellent time getting to her apartment. Zoe was a little heavy on the gas and it was interstate all the way. We were just glad that the cops weren't anywhere around.

"We'll, here we are!" announced Zoe as we pulled up the driveway to the complex. "I hope she's ready for us. We're a few minutes early."

"Thanks to your crazy driving," laughed Billie.

After looking around for a few minutes, we finally found her apartment and knocked on the door.

"Hey guys, I'm so glad you're finally here!" Jobella smiled, hugging each of us. "I really missed you all! Come on in!"

After all the greetings and hugs we sat down on her one sofa in her living room. She had bride's magazines and catalogues scattered all over her coffee table.

I glanced around her living room taking it all in. I had thought about moving into an apartment like this myself this next year while I was in school and maybe getting another girl to share expenses with me, so I was looking for ideas. This was an average size apartment with an open floor plan. She had a fireplace in the corner and above the mantle, she had a beautifully framed picture of her family. It had some wall art surrounding it in the form of birds and tree branches. She had a series of scented candles on the mantle. They were all lit, giving the apartment a soft aroma of flowers. The rest of the room seemed a little bare because she hadn't been in it all that long. and didn't have all her furniture yet. I guess she was waiting until her and Steve got married so they could furnish it together.

"Looks like someone is getting married around here," I laughed.

"Could be," She smiled back at me. "Now what made you guess that?"

She sure looked a lot better than she did when I saw her in that awful hospital room. When I saw her almost a year ago she was anorexic looking from not eating and her hair was cut in all kinds of crazy lengths and uncombed and dirty looking and she had scratch mark scars all over, including her face, and don't even get me started on that awful muumuu she had to wear. Now she was gorgeous, her scars were healed, she had a cute haircut, and she was bubbling over with happiness. She looked like one of those models in the magazines. I was so jealous of her!

The three of us spent the next two hours visiting and looking over the catalogues and magazines. We decided on the colors and gowns we were going to get and then we just visited for a while and ate the rest of the time we were there. There was so much to catch up on. We agreed to meet on Monday at David's Bridal after she got out of work to try on the dresses and make our final selections. We then spent some time looking on her laptop at the flower arrangements and wedding decorations she wanted to have. She was planning on having lilacs and calla lilies for the flowers and we could choose either a lilac or lavender color for our dresses. She explained that lilacs were her favorite flowers because it reminded her of the gardens at her home and the way her mom use to make bouquets out of them for their dining room table, so using them in her wedding would be in honor of her parents. The calla lilies would provide a contrast to the light purple by adding white and green to the bouquets and giving the bouquets a touch of elegance.

After we were through checking out all the wedding decorations on her laptop, Jobella starting talking about religion and we all started getting a little uncomfortable. When Jobella was in the hospital feeling sorry for herself, my two friends and I visited her at different times. With each one of us she acted like we were imposing on her and she was obviously upset by our visit. It was almost like she didn't want us to be there. She was angry that we waited so long to visit her. She thought we should've shown our concern sooner if we were her true friends. The fact was, all of us were uncomfortable seeing her in the state she was in. She was our friend and we were hurting for her. We thought that God was punishing her for whatever reason and caused all those things to happen to her. We tried to explain to her about God and how she needed to seek his forgiveness for her sins by praying, and doing good things. She reminded us that we were no better than she was, and even worse in most ways because we did a lot of things wrong. We tried to make things right again by going to her welcome home party at Steve's mom and dad's house when she got out of the hospital. We showed her that we still cared by surprising her with some new clothes we bought for her. It must have worked because now we are all still friends and here we are preparing to be her bridesmaids.

Now she was turning the tables on us. She said that God laid it on her heart to speak with us today. Essentially she said that it wasn't enough to be good and try to earn our way to heaven like we tried to tell her. We had to not only have a head knowledge of Christ and what he did for us when he was crucified for our sins, but we had to know him in our hearts, accept him, and live our lives for him.

I think, for myself, I knew what she was saying, but I couldn't quite grasp the concept of totally giving everything I had and felt over to Christ. I still had some wild oats to sow, and I believed my friends felt that way too. We still liked going out for drinks and fun with our other friends. We were all in college now and we all were experiencing total freedom for the first time. So yes, it would be an understatement to say that we all were uncomfortable with this conversation.

It was kind of weird, but just as Jobella was 'preaching' to us, a sudden severe thunderstorm came rolling in. It's not unusual for this type of weather late in the summer in North Carolina. A big bolt of lightning struck followed by a very loud crack of thunder. It hit just as she was talking, and bringing home a point. All of a sudden all the lights went out, and the candles on the mantle flickered. It felt very eerie, like God was trying to say something to us, but that was just plain crazy, right?

Still my friends and I came up with some lame excuse about why we needed to leave at just that moment. One of them said they had to be home in an hour, and I said that I had a hot date. All lies, of course. Don't get me wrong, we still all loved Jobella, and we're still her best friends, and we all wanted to be in her wedding, we just didn't want to get preached to that day.

Chapter 2

There were some ominous looking black thunderheads rolling across the sky as we were getting into Zoe's car. We hoped that we could beat the rain that was sure to come just as we drove back to Clairmonte, but as our luck would have it, there were a few large raindrops hitting our car even as we backed out of the driveway of Jobella's apartment complex.

As soon as we got on the interstate the heavens opened up and the torrential rains came. All of our cell phones started buzzing at once with weather alerts: 'Severe weather, flash flood warning, tornado watch all in effect for the next several hours' the warnings said.

I should have sat back in my seat, put my seat belt on, and prepare for a bad ride in this weather, but I was too interested in talking with my friends in the front seat to heed the voices in my head telling me to be smart and buckle up.

"We'll be fine, don't worry," Zoe said. "I've driven in a lot worse weather than this before. Remember, I've been commuting on this road on the weekends for over a year now, and I've gone through snow, ice, hail, hurricanes, all of it, and I never got in a wreck before. This SUV will get you where you want to go in spite of it all!"

Then to get our mind off the storm we were going through, we started talking about some of the comments Jobella made. "So what do you think about Jobella and what she was saying to us? Do you believe her?" Billie asked me, changing the subject.

"I'm not ready to give up my freedom yet. There's too much fun to be had. Lot's of parties at school, and my new boyfriend isn't a Christian. If I were to get all 'churchy' on him he would probably leave me. So no, maybe when I'm older and more settled down I'll think more about being the person God wants me to be. We're young and healthy. We still have time. How about you, Zoe?" I asked.

"I do believe in God and I am a Christian even though I don't always act like it. I know I should get back to church but right now I'm like you, I'm having too much fun. I know that God is going to save me, however, even though I don't always do the right things." Zoe replied.

Billie added. "Yep, me too. I'm 'born again' as they say. I definitely believe in Christ. I know he has my back when I need him. Everything is pretty much going good for me right now, so I don't guess I pray as much as I should lately. My Bible is getting a little dusty sitting on my shelf back home. I guess I should get it down, dust it off, and start reading it again."

"Jobella has really gotten to you two hasn't she?" I responded. "I swear, you two are so gullible to believe all this stuff. What has God done for you lately? Look at how good she always was and what happened to her. I'm almost afraid to be good. I don't want to be tested because everything is 'peachy keen' in my life, like it was for Jobella before everything fell apart for her."

"But look how good her life turned out. She is doing great now," Billie replied.

"She still lost her family! She's not ever getting her mom and dad back and who knows if she'll even see her brother and sister again. Sure she's getting married and has a gorgeous fiancé but it doesn't change the fact that she went through that ordeal and even she lost her faith in God while she was depressed," I answered.

Zoe turned to me. "Bad things happen to people, I get it, but we can't blame God for the bad. He loves us, and only wants what is best for us.

"You two believe what you want. I'm through with religion. I just don't have the faith that any of it is real anymore!"

All of a sudden Billie yelled. "Zoe, watch out, the traffic is slowing down up ahead, there must be an accident!"

Zoe was going too fast for the weather, and the traffic. She slammed on her brakes, and the car hydroplaned across the median into oncoming traffic going the other direction on the interstate. We all started screaming and the last thing I saw was the tractor-trailer coming straight at us. Then we heard the loud sound of metal against metal, crushing, screaming, cold wet metal swallowing us up along with shattering glass, and twisted metal penetrating our flesh. I still have nightmares about it to this day.

As the car slammed into the truck, I was thrown forward from my seat hitting my head on the dashboard, and my neck jerked unmercifully out of place. The last thing I heard and felt before blacking out was a loud popping sound in my neck and the sensation something like an electrical bolt going through my body. I blacked out, and the next thing I was aware of was the EMTs pulling me out of the twisted wreck and putting me on a stretcher. I heard them say something about guarding my neck. They thought that it might be broken because my head was turned at such a weird angle and I couldn't move anything. They immediately put a neck brace on me and straightened my arms and legs manually when they put me on the stretcher. It was strange, but other than a headache and a painful neck, I couldn't feel anything at all.

As I came to, I was aware of the sirens all around me. I recognized the different sounds of police cars, ambulances, and fire trucks. I saw all the flashing lights as they pulsated through the rain. The lights and sirens seemed so bright and loud to me. My head hurt so bad that they were intensified ten-fold. I heard the voices on the walkie-talkies relating the extent of the wreck. They were saying that all of the victims were alive, but one had to have CPR. They said they couldn't see how anyone could have survived the crash, as bad as the SUV looked. They said that only God could have saved us and that it was a miracle.

The local TV and radio stations found out about the wreck, and they were there quickly to report the news from the scene of the accident. How they got through the backed up traffic, I would never be able to figure out. I prayed that my parents would learn about it from the police and not by watching it on television. I didn't want my parents to see me like that and how bad the SUV looked.

Each of us, in turn, was taken from the wreck, loaded unto stretchers, and taken in separate ambulances to the trauma center at a nearby hospital.

News must have traveled pretty quickly because shortly after we arrived at the hospital all of our parents had come. We were all set up in different rooms to be examined. I overheard through the PA system a "code blue" being called. The first thing I thought of was Zoe. She must have crashed again. I sent up a quick prayer to God, if he was there, to protect her, and not let her die. Billie was in the ED room next to mine. The doctor was examining her. Evidently she had some broken bones because the nurse telephoned the orthopedic doctor who was on call. I heard her tell him that she had several broken bones, all on the left side. She must have been on the side of the vehicle that was hit on impact. Then I heard her scream out in pain as they were moving her leg and arm to x-ray them.

There was a lot of activity surrounding us. Doctor's and nurses were running about. They were pushing the crash cart down the hall to be used on Zoe. She had hit her head in the accident and they thought that she had a fractured skull and that the brain injury had resulted in her near death. After they stabilized her they rushed her to get a brain scan but they decided to go ahead and get a full body scan as well when they saw the dark bruises all over her body. The scan showed that she also had a few broken ribs either from the impact with the steering wheel or the intense CPR that was done on her two times already. One rib had pierced her heart and at least one of the other broken ribs tore a hole in her lung. Blood was pooling in her chest. She had to go immediately to surgery to repair all of the life threatening damage. If they didn't repair her heart quickly, she would bleed out and die.

When the extent of the broken bones in Billie was known she was also taken immediately to surgery.

All the parents were milling about in the hallways outside each of our areas. I could hear all of them sobbing, and questioning the doctors about all of our conditions and when they could see us. Billie and Zoe's parents were then led to a waiting area outside of surgery. They would remain there until her surgeries were over

A few minutes later they took me up to get an MRI of my head and neck. My Mom and Dad went with me holding my hand as we rolled down the hallway. I couldn't feel her touching my hand, but when Mom bent down to kiss my forehead as they were taking me to the radiology waiting area, I felt her tears falling on my cheek.

"Mom I'll be okay." I tried to reassure her as well as myself. "I'm really not hurting all that much, just my neck and head. Sounds like Zoe and Billie have it much worse than me, from the way it sounded in the ED."

"Yes, they didn't look very good, either. They have both gone to surgery." My mother replied.

"Ms. Eliza Goodman, we are ready for you now," called the technician, interrupting our conversation. "Mr. and Mrs. Goodman, you can wait out here until she's done, then we will be moving her to the ICU, and you can go be with her there. As soon as the doctor reads the report he will meet with you to discuss what he finds."

As they were doing the MRI, I thought about my friends. I prayed that if there was a God that he would be with them and that they would be okay during surgery. I really didn't expect an answer to that prayer, but it was a comfort to say it, just in case he did exist.

Chapter 3

I woke up later that evening after sleeping the rest of the afternoon. My mother and father were sitting by my bed in the ICU in tears. I tried to turn my head toward them but I had a ridged neck brace on so that I couldn't move my head. I was laying flat on my back. They wouldn't even allow me to put my head on a pillow. I called to my mother to come closer so I could see her without trying to turn my head

"Mom, what did the test show?" I asked her.

"It looks like you had a concussion and there was some kind of shadow around your spinal cord in your neck. It's inconclusive at this time, and we have to wait for the swelling to go down before they can determine if you have a broken neck or not."

My mother was a nurse, so I knew that she understood everything the doctor told her and she in turn would tell it to me straight. She was very clinical that way and I didn't want her to spare my feelings. Dad was an architect and the only medical jargon that he knew was what he learned from my mother. She had worked with patients that had spinal cord injuries before and she knew the prognosis of someone who had a broken neck was poor. She wasn't surprised when I told her that I had no feelings below my neck.

"Who is taking care of Jamie while you all are here?" I asked suddenly remembering my little brother. He was five years old now and a little livewire. He was one of mom and dad's little "surprises". They were in their early forties and didn't think that they would ever have another child when she became pregnant with him. He's been a joy to all of us ever since. He was a real cutie and the love of my life. Jamie was getting ready to go to kindergarten in the fall. He spent the days now in daycare while Mom and Dad were working.

"Your grandmother is watching him. She's going to let him spend the rest of the weekend with her, so we can stay right here with you all night and tomorrow if we need to."

"I don't know what you can do for me right now. I'm not going anywhere that's for sure."

"Well we can always give you moral support and a sip of water now and again."

"That actually sounds pretty good right now, the drink of water I mean."

I couldn't raise my head because of the brace and I tried to lift my arm to my face, but it wouldn't budge. I couldn't even move my little finger. It felt like someone had tied me down, that is, if I were actually able to feel anything.

"Mom!" I cried out. "I can't move! What's going on? My body feels so strange. I'm looking down at it and it doesn't feel like it belongs to me. I'm totally numb!"

"The doctor's think you may have some spinal cord damage," she said sadly. "They say that once the swelling goes down they may be able to determine if the damage is going to be permanent, or if there is something they can do about it."

"Do you mean I'm going to be like this the rest of my life?"

"Only time will tell. We hope not, but we have to be ready to accept whatever the outcome is," she replied.

"We will make sure that you get the best help we can get for you, Eliza, no matter what the cost," Dad added. "We're going to be here for you, princess."

I started to cry then. I didn't want to be this way. Not then and especially not forever. What kind of life would I have if I were to be paralyzed for the rest of my life? Why didn't I heed caution and put on my seat belt. Would it have made a difference in my outcome? After all, Zoe and Billie had theirs on, but they were still really messed up.

My mother wiped the perspiration from my face and gave me a sip of water, which I immediately started choking on. When I couldn't quit coughing and started turning blue my mother rang for the nurse.

"What are you doing, Mrs. Goodman? She isn't to eat or drink anything by mouth while she is laying flat on her back. You should know better than that! You're a nurse for goodness sake!" As she fussed at mom, I continued to cough. She hooked up the suction machine quickly and ran a long thin tube down my throat to get out any excessive liquid that was going down into my lungs. I heard the gurgling from the suction and I started coughing because of the tube being forced down my throat. It made me start choking worse. After they pulled it out, I stopped coughing, but I was still looking bluish, so they put an oxygen mask on me. The nurse took my water pitcher away from my bedside, and filled it with ice chips.

"If she gets thirsty again just give her these ice chips, one at a time. It's too difficult for her to swallow laying flat on her back. She's going to continue getting IV fluids and electrolytes until they can put a feeding tube into her stomach. With the IV's, she shouldn't need to drink anything, just something to keep her mouth moist. She'll more than likely need IV's, and a feeding tube until she is better and can feed herself, or if she remains paralyzed, is able to sit up, and have someone else feed her."

All of those options sounded horrible! If I could, I would kill myself right now! *'God if you're up there, please just let me die now!'* I prayed silently to myself. I wouldn't dare say those words aloud and let my mom and dad know how I really felt!

Mom and Dad stayed with me all night that first night. They had to sleep outside in the ICU waiting room away from the patients. The nurses wouldn't allow visitors in the unit during the night when the patients were trying to sleep, but my parents wanted to be there in case there were any changes in my condition.

As I lay there in the prison of my body, I thought about everything that happened that day. Why did I not listen to Jobella? Why did we insist on leaving right at that moment? We should have stayed until the storm passed, then we wouldn't all be here in the hospital on the brink of death or severely maimed. In hindsight, it wouldn't have hurt us to stay and at least hear her out. At least she had peace now after her ordeal, and a fully restored life. All I had now was a body that no longer worked. Even if God was real, and wanted to use me, what good could I do in this body? My brain was still functioning, but I couldn't act on anything that could be useful in this body.

I couldn't go to sleep that night. In the darkness in the ICU, it seemed like there were a million tiny lights blinking like so many electronic stars, all signaling the treachery in the rest of the beds on the unit. Billie and Zoe were just a few beds over from where I was lying. I couldn't turn my head to look at them, but I knew they were there because I heard the nurses discuss their care in their night shift report.

Zoe was still fighting for her life and still in a coma, I heard them say. They also said that they didn't know if she would make it through the night. While they were sharing their report, right on cue her heart monitor started alarming. Her heart had stopped beating again. They called a "code blue" and all of a sudden there were doctors and nurses everywhere! *'Lord, if you are there,'* I prayed frantically to myself, *'please help my friend. I know I don't deserve your help but Zoe does. She loves you.'*

They were afraid to do chest compressions on her because of her broken ribs, but they had no choice. I heard the defibrillator charge up several times, and then zap her over and over again. They finally got her heart to start beating, but during the ordeal I thought my own heart would stop. My heart was breaking for my two friends.

I heard Billie crying. She was in the bed next to Zoe. She was pretty beat up with all her broken bones. Both her left leg and arm were in casts and were suspended by traction. They had to put pins and rods in her leg because her bones were so shattered they had to piece them all together. She rang out for some pain medication and the nurse took it to her. I'm sure she was aware of what was going on with Zoe, as well, and was as scared for her as I was for Zoe and myself.

I realized then that my affliction was a blessing in disguise. I wasn't really in any kind of pain because I could feel nothing from my neck down. I actually had several cuts and bruises all over my body, but I couldn't feel them and I was also alive and awake, not in a coma like Zoe. I was aware, for better or worse, of everything that was going on around me, and I internalized the shear misery of everyone on the ward, especially for my friends.

When I couldn't settle down and relax after the drama and concern for my friends, I rang for the nurse to see if I could get something to help me fall to sleep. She had to give me something in my IV because of my not being able to swallow pills. The medicine took effect quickly and I didn't know anything else until the morning.

I learned the next morning that Zoe did make it through the code blue, but it was the third time in twenty-four hours that they had to do CPR on her. I didn't know how much more she could take, or how much damage was done to her brain and body after going through so much trauma and lack of oxygen.

It was all a waiting game now, for all three of us…

Chapter 4

The next day they moved me to a private room on the intermediate unit. They felt like I was stable enough and out of danger to warrant my being moved. I think they noticed how upset I became when I was listening to the drama in the ICU, especially with Zoe and Billie, during the night.

Mom and Dad said that they would need to go home for a change of clothes and a shower after they moved me into a room. They would be picking my brother up from my grandmother's house, and they would bring him by to see me. I really didn't want him to see me like this, but I did want to see him. If anyone could make me smile, he could.

After they were gone, the nursing assistants came in to bathe me. It was so embarrassing to have strangers look at my body like that and clean me up after my messes. They were very discreet when they were bathing me, but I still felt uncomfortable. They had to be extra careful not to bend my back and neck and had to logroll me to get to my backside. Logrolling meant that they had to turn me over in one motion. It took three of them to do it effectively. They had to keep my back straight, and not let it twist at all. One person was at my head holding my head and neck straight with the rest of my spine, another person was at my hips, and the third moved my legs. It was terrible to not be able to do anything for myself. So many things I use to take for granted, like bathing, eating, dressing, and even going to the bathroom, I was no longer able to do for myself. After they bathed me the doctor said that they could try to put me up at a slight ten-degree angle in the bed, if I was able to tolerate it, so I could watch television, or look at my visitors when they came in. My back and neck still had to be kept straight, however, but it was nice to be able to see something again besides the ceiling. Unfortunately that didn't last long because later that morning they would move me into the intermediate care unit, and unto a special bed called a Stryker frame bed. It was a specially made bed for people with broken necks.

Later in the morning, before they moved me, a physical therapist came into my room and introduced himself as Eric Evans. He was really nice looking, and I knew that if I had to have physical therapy, he would be someone I could like helping me. He had brown hair, and beautiful blue eyes, and a smile that would make a dead person feel better.

"Well, good morning, Ms. Goodman. How are you doing today?" He asked.

"How would you be feeling if you had been hit by an eighteen wheeler yesterday?"

"I'd say, I'd be glad I can't feel anything from my neck down, but it's a shame you can't move anything either, though. You don't mind if I go through a little of your background with you and get to know you a little better, do you? I'm going to be a sort of personal trainer for you and it helps if I know a little bit about you, and what your expectations are."

"I'm glad to have someone that cares that much, even if it is just your job to do so."

"But I do care. I can't imagine what you're going through right now, but we're going to do the best we can to help you. Okay, about getting to know each other, let's start over from the beginning. A little bit about me first. I'm Eric. I've just started working here a little over a year ago. I graduated from Duke with a masters degree in sports medicine and physical therapy, last year."

"Really? I go to Duke too! Well at least I did before this happened. I've been trying to decide what to major in. I was actually there on a sports scholarship for my track and field abilities. I won a lot of championships, but it doesn't look like I'm going to be able to do that anymore. I'll be happy just to be able to walk again."

"Well don't get too discouraged. Your accident was just yesterday. We might be able to help you out. You just never know."

"You look awfully young. Do you mind if I ask how old you are?" I asked.

"Wow, we are getting personal now," he laughed. "I'm twenty-five. I know what you're thinking. I'm too young to have a master's degree. I actually graduated early. Now, how about if we get a little pumped, and get into some range of motion exercises."

As we went back and forth with the small talk, he was moving my arms and legs in all sorts of directions. I couldn't help but watch him as he did his job. Once in a while he would look at me and grin. He had a really cute smile. If I was healthy and able to be out of here I could really go for someone like him and I definitely would try to snatch him up. But as is stands now, I'm just another statistic of a pathetic case, and a client that needs working on.

When he bent over to pick up my leg to move it around, a dog tag with a cross on it that he was wearing around his neck, fell outside of his scrub top.

"I couldn't help but notice your dog tag. Are you a Christian?" I asked.

"I sure am. I couldn't do my job if I didn't have faith in God's healing power."

"I thought I was too, but my friend, convinced me that I really wasn't and that I just had a head knowledge of God. My friends and I were actually at her house yesterday, and was going over plans for her wedding. It was on the way home from her apartment that we got in the car wreck. She was trying to talk with us about the real meaning of being a Christian. I think my friends got more out of her preaching than I did, I'm afraid."

"I saw that wreck on TV. I can't believe that you all weren't killed!"

"That's what everyone says. That it was a miracle," I frowned. "So take a good look at your 'miracle girl' you're working on. My two friends are in ICU. One of them coded three different times in the last twenty-four hours and is in a coma and the other one is really busted up."

"Still, you all are alive, and where there is life there is hope, right?"

"I suppose." I frowned.

"Well, I'm finished for today, but I'll be with you everyday about this time," he smiled. "Think about what your friend said, okay? It's a lot easier to work with a patient that has a positive attitude and believes she can get better."

"Okay, I'll try. I will definitely look forward to your visits each day." I smiled.

He laughed when I said that. He's probably heard that from a lot of young women.

After he left they brought a tray of food in to me. "I'm going to try to feed you, Ms. Goodman. Now that you are partially sitting up, the doctor thought that we could try and see if you would be able to tolerate it. My name is Cindy, by the way, I don't think I told you my name this morning when my co-worker and I were bathing you."

It was a bit awkward when she was trying to feed me. I only took small bites because I was afraid of choking again. I felt like she was trying to rush me, and I suddenly became afraid. After a few bites I told her I was finished. I didn't want anything else.

A few minutes later my doctor came in to see me. I told him about my morning and how uncomfortable I was with eating. My neck hurt a little more in the angled position as well. He decided that I should go get another MRI. A little while after he left, some technicians came from the radiology department and put me on a special stretcher that could go through the MRI machine. It took three of them to move me, one to hold my head straight, one at my upper back, and one under my legs, just like the aides did earlier. They rolled me over, and slid a board under me, and pulled me off the bed unto the stretcher. Even though they were careful I still could feel a grating sensation at the base of my neck.

The MRI was the same as I had when I first got to the hospital. The loud clanging sound from the machine made my headache worse and I longed for it to get over with.

When I got back to my room, my mom, dad, and Jamie were all there waiting on me. I wanted to reach out to hug them, especially my little brother, but of course I couldn't. Mom and Dad kissed me on my cheek, and whispered that they loved me. Jamie held back, hiding behind them and I could tell he wanted to cry.

He hugged Mom. "What's wrong with 'Liza, Mom? Why is she laying like that? How come she's not moving?"

"She hurt her neck, Jamie. She has to hold real still so it will get better." She replied.

"Can I touch her?"

"Sure, just be careful. If you want to, you can kiss her cheek like we did." With that he got as close as he could. He laid his little arm across my chest and kissed me on the cheek.

"I love you, 'Liza, I want you to get better and come home."

"I'm going to do my best to get well real soon, Jamie. You be good for Mom and Dad while I'm in here, okay?"

After they had been visiting for a little while, Dr. Anderson came in to give the MRI results to us. "I'm afraid I have some bad news, Eliza. We were able to see the damage more clearly in this MRI this morning. It does look like you have suffered a broken neck. It looks like there is damage to the fifth and sixth cervical vertebrate and a partial tear to your spinal cord. We are going to have to operate to fuse your vertebrate together later on, but we need to wait until the swelling goes down further, and it has a chance to mend on it's own. This afternoon we are going to place a clamp on your head so we can put your head and neck in traction to separate the damaged vertebrate, and allow the spinal cord to heal as much as possible, and prevent further damage. I'm also going to put you on a special bed that will allow the nurses to turn you every two hours without actually disturbing your spine and neck. You will need to be turned that often to prevent you from getting bedsores. You will have to be in this bed and have the traction for at least six weeks. While you continue to be in this bed we will be placing a tube through your abdominal wall, and into your stomach, and you will receive nutrition that way. Eating and drinking while you are lying flat is totally out of the question. We will also put a catheter into your bladder so that you won't need to worry about being put on the bedpan so often. After the six weeks are up, we should be able to do surgery to fuse the broken bones of your neck together to protect what's left of your spinal cord. Then we'll put a brace on your neck like the one you have on now until you heal from your surgery. After the operation we will gradually increase your activity up to, and including being able to sit in a wheel chair, and then we can do more intense physical and occupational therapy."

"When are you going to do this?" I asked for the three of us.

"We'd like to do the procedure for your head traction and feeding tube as soon as possible. There is a special room here on the unit that we do minor surgical procedures in. We'll take you there. It's probably good that you didn't eat so much breakfast, Eliza, as I would like to get this done this afternoon, the sooner the better. The nurse told me about you not eating much because you were afraid of getting choked. That was probably a wise unintentional move on your part," he smiled.

"Is it going to hurt much?" I asked.

"We are going to sedate you so you won't feel too much and we will give you a local anesthetic for your head areas where we will be drilling the holes. While we have you in there we are also going to put in what we call a g-tube through your abdominal wall and into your stomach and a Foley catheter in your bladder. Those things won't hurt at all since you don't have any feeling below your neck. After we do all that we will be putting you in a special bed. We have a room all set up for spinal cord injuries like yours. It is larger than our regular rooms because the staff needs to be able to get around the bed to turn you over. Also there are special mirrors placed in strategic places so you will be able to watch television and speak to visitors without turning or lifting your head."

"All of that sounds really painful."

"You'll have some pain from the head wounds for a couple of days but after that it won't bother you all that much. Remember you can always request pain meds if you need them."

"Doctor, will there be anyone there to see after her when she needs something?" asked my mother.

"The nurses and aides will be checking on her frequently, especially for the first twenty-four hours after her procedure. Remember they have to turn her in the frame bed every two hours anyway and post surgically, they have to do vital signs at least every hour. There's also a special form that they have to fill out every time they turn her and check her blood pressure and pulse, so they are held accountable for her care."

"Could I stay with her for the first few weeks? I could get some time off from work if you need me too." Mom asked.

"That won't be necessary. It will be hard for you to stay twenty-four-seven. You'll wear yourself out and Eliza might not like you hovering over her all that time. You can see her after work, and they will let you spend the night occasionally if you wish. That should be more than sufficient if you're willing to do that but even that really isn't necessary. We have excellent staff on this unit. By the way, don't you work here in the hospital?"

"Yes, I work on the cardiac floor. I guess I can see her during my lunch break and after work, and on my days off. I probably shouldn't be using up all my sick time anyway and they are so short staffed already."

"So Eliza, are you good with that?" asked the doctor turning towards me.

"I am. I'm dreading the minor surgery I'm getting ready to have, though. Can my family stay until after I'm put in my 'torture chamber'?" I joked.

"By all means. Sounds good. Well, it looks like they are getting ready to take you back now and I have to go get prepped. This really won't take too long. I shouldn't think more than an hour at the most. Mr. and Mrs. Goodman, you might want to go to the cafeteria to get something to eat while you're waiting."

I had tears in my eyes as they left. I was afraid of what they were getting ready to do to me, but as much as I tried to put a brave front on, I couldn't help but show how scared I was.

"Sounds like a good idea. We will see you in a little while, Eliza. We love you," Dad said, putting his hand on my shoulder and kissing me on the forehead. "We'll always be here for you, princess. We won't be going anywhere."

Chapter 5

The doctors and nurses were already in the small procedure room when they rolled me in. They gathered around me with their gowns, gloves, and masks in place. They gave me a shot in my IV that was supposed to calm me down enough to relax me and put me to sleep. Then they proceeded to shave my head so they would have a clear area to prep my head for the anesthetic and the drilling. Before my accident, I had prided myself in having beautiful long dark hair. It upset me that they were going to shave it all off. The only good part of it would be that since I wouldn't be able to do anything to take care of my hair, it would be easier for the aides and nurses to care for my scalp without my hair getting in the way.

I suddenly became afraid when I saw the large clamp that they would be embedding in my skull and then I saw the long hypodermic needle that held the local anesthetic, but the object that really scared me was the drill. It looked just like the one that dad used in his workshop. Thankfully, the medication finally started to take effect and I became really sleepy and it no longer bothered me about what they were getting ready to do. Just as I was drifting off I felt the liquid from the cleansing agent they swabbed above my ear drip down behind my ears to my neck. I cried out when I felt the sharp sting of the needle used for the local anesthetic that they administered on each side of my head. While they were waiting for it to take effect, they cleansed a small area on my abdomen, and made a slit with a scalpel, and then afterwards they cut a small hole in my stomach, and placed a tube directly into it, and then closed it up with sutures. That tube would be there until I was able to eat again. They placed another tube into my bladder. After all that was done and the numbing medicine started taking effect, the doctor would start drilling the holes in my skull. He had cut small slits in my skin to expose my skull, and then started drilling. I really didn't feel it, but the sound was unnerving. It was so close to my ears, it sounded extremely loud and I could feel the vibrations as my skull bones were being grated down. They sutured the head wounds closed with the clamp imbedded in both sides of my skull. I was worried that it would accidently come out, but the doctor assured me that it wasn't going anywhere.

After they were through with my procedure they rolled me in the room with the strangest looking bed I've ever seen. It had a bottom mattress with canvas straps and a top mattress frame that would fit on top of me so that when it came time to turn me over they would lower that over me and buckle me in and turn my whole body upside down. In the upper mattress there was a hole where my face would fit when I was on my stomach. The whole point of the bed was to keep my body as straight as possible, and my neck in proper alignment. There was a weight hanging at the top of the bed that would be attached to the clamp on my head. The head traction was to keep my cervical vertebrate in alignment and separated, so that the bones could have a chance to heal and not put more pressure on my spinal cord. By turning my whole body every two hours, it would hopefully keep me from getting pressure sores. It wasn't the most comfortable position to be in, but it could have been worst. I could have felt the discomfort all over, but since I had no feeling it really didn't bother me. Only my head and neck continued to hurt because of the traction.

Mom, Dad, and Jamie came back after they ate lunch. I wasn't much in the mood for company, so they made their visit short. All I wanted was to get something for pain, and just take a nap, that is if I could get rid of my headache from the pain of my head wounds.

We all agreed that it would probably be best to let me alone for the rest of the day, and so they went home.

The nurses and aides came in frequently the rest of the day, just as the doctor said they would, to make sure my feeding tube and catheter were working properly, and to turn me in my bed. It was more uncomfortable laying flat on my stomach. There was a hole in the mattress where my face would fit and I could see the floor beneath me. A sling across the hole would hold my head in place. There were mirrors under the bed that would reflect the television in the room so if I wanted to, I could watch television from that position. There was a soft call bell on the sling under my face so if I needed something, I could tap it with my nose. They sure thought of everything.

I finally fell asleep and rested peacefully the rest of the night. I didn't even wake up when they came in to rotate the bed.

The next day the doctor came in and checked on me and on the incisions that were made the day before. He changed my dressings and said that everything was looking good. He did have me on antibiotics, however, to prevent infections at my wound sites. The bruises that I got in the wreck were turning into shades of purple and yellow now. I didn't have a chance to look in any mirrors to see how bad I looked between the bruising that must have been on my face and neck from the accident and shaved head from the surgery. I could only imagine how horrible I must have looked. I dreaded seeing anyone outside my family and staff and I prayed that it would be a few days before any of my friends came.

Eric came in to do some range of motion exercises with me. I was happy to see him, but I hoped he wasn't put off by the way I looked.

"Good morning, Eliza. I'm here to do some range of motion exercises with you," he smiled.

"I didn't think you could do anything with me while I'm in this crazy bed."

"Well, I can't take you out dancing, or anything like that." He laughed. "But we can do some exercises as long as they don't mess with your spinal cord."

I was lying on my back while he gently bent each arm at the elbow. He laid one hand on my shoulder and the other on my hand. Then he would move each of my fingers and wrists.

"I can feel your hand on my shoulders!" I cried out. "I can't feel anything else, but I can feel that!"

"That's great, that's a sign that we may be able to do some arm and hand training once you get out of this bed and traction. Sometimes if the breaks in the neck are low enough down you can still have some movement and feeling in the upper part of your body. That's a good thing. Later on when you are able to get up, we can work on that, okay?"

"That sounds good. I just wish I could do something now."

"With this type of injury, you're going to have to develop a lot of patience. None of it is going to be easy."

Shortly after Eric left, Mom came in to see me. She must have been on her lunch break. She was carrying a gorgeous bouquet of flowers and several cards. There was a table beside my bed that was slightly higher than the bed so I could see them without turning my head. The bouquet was a combination of roses and daisies. Who knew those two flowers would make such a pretty combination.

"Who are the flower's from, Mom?"

"They are from Jeremy. He brought them to the house after I told him what happened to you. He said he would try to get by and see you in a few days after things settle down a little bit and you felt like visitors."

Jeremy and I have been dating for a little more than a month. I met him during one of my summer school classes at Duke. He was the total jock package. We were taking a physical science class together and being as we were both athletes, we hit it right off. He was planning on going into coaching after he finished school, if the pros didn't draft him first, that is. He was handsome, muscular and my kind of guy. Since football season hadn't started back yet, we spent a lot of our dates going out partying, and taking in the nightclub scene. He definitely liked to party, but once the season started all that would have to be curtailed. His coach was all about his team being clean and sober. They would be back in training and clean living next week. He probably wouldn't be able to come and see me much after football season started he told me.

"So who are all the cards from?"

"There are a few from the nurses I work with and a few from the ladies at the church we use to go to and one from your friend, Jobella. Some of them would like to come visit you, but I told them that they should wait for a few days, and let you get settled in."

She read each of the cards to me, and everyone wished me the best, and of course they had to include something about trusting in God, that he would heal me, and so on.

"Thanks, Mom. You can set them up on the table where I can see them."

After Mom had left and my therapy was over, it was time to be turned on my stomach again. After they flipped me over the nurse checked my skin over to make sure everything was still intact and no redness was present. The aide cleaned me up and massaged some lotion on me and covered me with a blanket. I was able to feel the massage over my upper back and shoulders. It felt wonderful. I was finally able to settle down for a nap the rest of the afternoon.

Life was pretty much the same over the next several weeks. Everything became predictable and routine. The nursing staff was in and out every two hours to flip me over and do skin care. I felt like a rotisserie chicken being flipped and basted. When my tube feeding finished, they would hang a new bag. When my catheter bag was full they emptied it out, and when I made messes, they cleaned me up, and of course, my therapy. That was pretty much my life now.

I spent my leisure time watching television via my mirrors. I got pretty good at some of the game shows. I could answer most of the questions on 'Jeopardy' and 'Who Wants to be a Millionaire' and I got hooked on at least one soap opera.

My mom was as good as her word and came down to eat her lunch in my room when she was at work. She brought me any mail and cards that I received and read them all to me. After work she would come by to make sure that everyone was treating me all right and to do little things for me. After a while she stopped staying the night, because there really wasn't anything else she could do for me.

Chapter 6

A couple weeks after I got the flowers from Jeremy, he decided to finally come and visit me. I could tell from his look that he wasn't expecting to see me this way. He stayed close to the door. He looked very uncomfortable and looked like he wanted to bolt out.

"Hi, Eliza, when they told me that you were hurt in a car wreck, I wanted to come and see you, but your Mom said to wait a few days until you were settled. I figured by now you'd be up in a wheel chair and ready to go home. I had no idea I'd find you like this!"

"Well, this is what I look like now. Stuck in this torture chamber. I can't move, or feel anything from my neck down."

"Are you ever going to get better?"

"I'll be able to get up into a wheelchair after surgery, but they are pretty sure I won't ever be able to walk again, or maybe not even able to use my arms. I'm sorry, but I can't turn my head to look at you. Can you come closer? I promise I won't bite and I'm not contagious or anything. I have to see you with mirrors unless you are standing right over me, or come close enough, so I can turn my eyes to see you."

"I'm sorry, I was just shocked to see you this way." He finally came close to me, and kissed me on my forehead. "Does that head thing hurt? It looks painful."

"I'm kind of getting use to it now. The headaches are going away. They are going to keep it on me until my neck bones, and my spinal cord have a chance to heal some, and then they will do surgery."

"How long will that be?"

"I have about another month to be here in this type of bed. After surgery they will move me to a regular bed and then begin trying to get me in a wheelchair."

"That's quite a long time. You'll probably have several months of therapy after that and then you still may not be any better?"

"That's about the size of it. Can you handle that? Where does not leave us?"

"I'm sorry, but I don't think I'm up for having to deal with a crippled girlfriend. No offense, but I'm not the kind of boyfriend you need right now. I do wish you all the best, though and I hope everything works out for you."

After he walked out the door, my eyes burned with my tears. What did I expect anyway, that he would express his undying, sacrificial love for me? I didn't blame him for walking out, not really, if the role were reversed, I probably would have done the same thing.

Later when my Mom walked in, I told her what happened with Jeremy.

"He's a jerk anyway, Eliza. I never liked him much. You can do so much better than him, even in your condition. He just proved to you how shallow he really is! I wouldn't waste another minute crying over the likes of him."

"I suppose you're right, but who is ever going to love me like this!"

"If God wills it, there will be someone. If not, then it was never meant to be."

"Thanks for your comfort, but truly, I can't trust God to dictate anything in my life right now. If he wanted what was best for me, I wouldn't be here in this shape, in the first place!"

"I've worked with a lot of patients with spinal cord injuries through the years. Some just give up, but then there were those that overcame their circumstances and came out of it as better people than they were before and are great contributors to society. There are even some with your injury that get married and have children. It is still possible. It's just your skeletal muscles that aren't working but your other bodily functions still continue to work as before."

"That's good to know, but I still don't think any guy is going to be attracted to me now."

"The right guy will love you more for your mind and your heart. If he doesn't love you for all your good qualities, he's not worth loving. To be perfectly honest, I'm glad Jeremy broke up with you. He wasn't the type of guy that deserves you. You need someone who can love you for yourself."

"They are attracted to the package before they look at the ingredients." I quipped. "Look at Jeremy, when I wasn't the pretty little thing he expected to see, he couldn't wait to get out of here."

"It just goes to show how shallow he really was. Guy's like him like to play the field and not just the football field. They have girls hanging all over them. It would have only been time before he went on to the next girl after you. I wouldn't be surprised if he didn't already have another one waiting on him."

"You are sure encouraging, aren't you, Mom? I'm sure you're right and you are making me feel a little better, thanks for that.

I'll keep it in mind when all the guys start flirting with me and lining up at my door to ask me out." I smiled.

After supper Mom came back with Dad, and Jamie. Jamie hadn't been in to see me for over a week. Mom thought that it would cheer me up to see my little brother again. Sure enough it did.

"Hi 'Liza, I missed you!" He said as he ran up to me and threw his arms around my shoulders and kissed me on the cheek.

I could feel his arms on my shoulders and it seemed good to be touched my sweet little brother. "I drew a picture of you. I brought it. You want to see it?"

"Sure that would be great. You are a wonderful little artist!"

It was a picture of me laying in a space ship with a helmet on my head. I guess he must of thought my bed looked like a spacecraft, and my headgear looked like a helmet.

"Very funny." I laughed. "You have a good imagination."

"Read the back 'Liza." He turned it over and held it in front of my face. It said 'I Love you 'Liza. Please get well soon'.

"I love you too, Jamie. You are the best little brother a girl could ever have. You are officially my number one guy! I wish I could hug you right now."

"Hey, what about me?" asked Dad.

"You don't count. You have to love me! You're stuck with me no matter what shape I'm in. Besides, have you made me a card? All my boyfriends have to make me a card!" I smiled.

"I'll have to remember that the next time I come. I promise I'll make you a card, but keep in mind it will have to be a picture of a building."

"I'll take that, after all, that's all architects know how to draw, right?" I laughed.

"You'd be surprised what we architects can do if we put our mind to it for the ones we love."

"Awe, I love you Dad. You are a wonderful father. You and Mom are the best parent's I could ask for, and you must have done something right because you love Jamie and me so much."

Mom and Dad lifted my spirits that night, but I was still having trouble going to sleep. It continued to upset me about Jeremy and his reaction to seeing me like this. Mom and Dad and my little brother were great, but I worried that no one else would ever love me. What guy would want to deal with this? What if I never experienced a true physical and heartfelt love of a man again? As I lay there I thought of the last time that Jeremy held me, and I felt his caresses, and the warmth of his kisses on my neck, and the passion we had for each other. I wept knowing that I may never get to feel that again.

I finally went to sleep, but not before the nurse gave me medication to help me rest.

Chapter 7

The next morning started out like every other day in my sad existence. The nursing assistant came in to give me my bed bath. I was already on my stomach, so she started with my back and when she was through she laid a fresh sheet over me. After she flipped me to my back she washed the rest of me. What I wouldn't give to be able to stand in a shower or soak in a tub. Would that day ever come again?

No sooner had she finished and then Eric came in. "Good morning sunshine" He said.

"What's so good about it?" I asked.

"God gave us a beautiful day to be alive. Don't you feel it?" With that he flung the curtains open and the bright sunshine flowed in. "I dare you to be grumpy now!"

"The only good thing about today is that you walked through that door!" I tried to smile. "Where were you yesterday?"

"Can't a guy get a day off once in a while?" he smiled.

"Not when you have to work with me," I replied, smiling back at him. "You're not allowed a day off, I'm too high maintenance."

"You've got that right!" He laughed. I'm here now, so let's get cracking. I got to get you quick before 'Nurse Ratchet' comes in to flip her burger."

"Are you implying that I'm just a piece of meat?"

"Wouldn't think of implying that at all! You are a gorgeous girl that has a lot going for her. You just have to discover how much you really do have to give!"

"Well, I don't know if you warmed up the rest of my muscles, but my face sure feels a lot hotter right now!" I said.

He grinned again at me and started his therapy by moving my arms in a circle from the shoulders and then worked his way down my arms to my elbows, and then my wrists, and fingers. He worked my legs by grabbing my foot and bending my leg at the knee several times and then worked my ankle and toes. When he was through, he started doing my opposite side. I couldn't feel anything he was doing, except my upper arms. I closed my eyes and imagined what each movement felt like.

"Are you doing okay?" He asked.

"So far, are my joints staying limber? I don't want my arms and legs getting stiff and curled up."

"As long as you have some one to do this everyday, even after you go home, that shouldn't happen."

"Can I take you home with me when I leave here?" I asked, only half joking this time. I actually wouldn't mind that at all.

"Your mom and dad may have something to say about that!" He laughed.

"They won't mind, I promise."

After he left I had mixed feelings about him. Eric was such a nice guy. I could really like him as a boyfriend. At the same time I was sad because I knew that after he left me he'd be moving on to other patients. I was just one of his many cases and I'm sure he talked with other people like he talked with me. I'm sure it was just part of his job to be nice.

At lunchtime Mom came to see me as usual. She had stopped by Billie and Zoe's rooms and wanted to catch me up on the latest concerning my two friends.

"Well," she said, "look's like Billie is going home this week. She's still in her arm and leg casts and she'll have to be in a wheelchair until she heals because she can't use a walker or crutches. It's going to be pretty awkward for her to get around. Her mom and dad will have to take her everywhere, and she'll have to be lifted into and out of the car."

"You'll have to do that with me too, if I ever get out of here, that is."

"But you won't have a heavy cast on your arm and leg. It will be extremely hard to maneuver her. It will be a little easier with you. I understand she's planning on going to Jobella's wedding this coming weekend."

"Oh, that's right, I almost forgot about them. I wonder why she hasn't come by to see me."

"I thought she did come by. I understand that you weren't very nice to her when you saw her."

"I must have been out of it because I don't remember that, or seeing her."

"She did call me the other day to find out how you were doing and I gave her a few details. She said that her and Steve would try to get by and see you after their wedding and honeymoon. They're going on a cruise."

"Lucky them. It must be nice to be well, happy, and in love. I couldn't be happier for them. I just wish it was me!"

"Anyway, Billie said that she would come to visit you when she get's ready to leave."

"So, how's Zoe doing?

"She's still in ICU. She semi-comatose now but she's trying to wake up, but doesn't quite get fully awake. Her brain monitor is showing a little more activity. They don't know yet how she'll be when she wakes up. They're worried about brain damage since she went without oxygen for so long because of her three codes."

"That's so sad for her. I hope she's going to be okay. She and Billie are such sweet people, and good friends to me. I wish I could see them."

"I'm sure they'll come by when they're able. Your Dad and I got you something. We'll bring it by tonight when we visit."

"Did Dad make that get well card for me, yet? Is that what the surprise is?"

"Can't tell you, or it won't be a surprise."

As I laid there the remainder of the day, I fell asleep thinking about everything I was missing. I dreamt of the last time I was running through the woods practicing for a cross-country marathon. I could feel the power in my legs as I ran and the heat of my muscles in my thighs as they were stretching with each step. I could feel the moss under my feet, cushioning my steps as I landed each one. My arms were swinging in cadence with my legs and my heart was beating hard and fast. My breaths were strong and my lungs felt healthy as I breathed in deeply and the oxygen from the air was flowing through my blood stream. The endorphins were surging in my body making me feel truly alive. Running was the best medicine in the world. I felt at one with the universe after a run like that. As I sat on a fallen tree to rest a bit, I listened to the birds calling back and forth to each other and I heard a woodpecker tapping at a nearby oak tree trying to get at some dinner. I saw the beautiful pink blooms of the mountain laurel all around me and I savored the beauty of the forest.

"Eliza, wake up." I heard someone say, waking me up from my beautiful dream.

Sitting in a wheelchair next to my bed was my friend Billie. "Hi Eliza. I wanted to drop by and see how you are doing before I go home. I may not be able to see you again for a while. It's going to be really awkward getting in and out of our van, so I doubt if I'll be able to get out much. How are you coping with everything?"

"There is not much coping, I just have to lay here at the mercy of everyone that's taking care of me. I can't really get in any trouble. It's tough not being able to do anything."

"Do the doctor's think that you will get better?"

"They are going to do surgery in a few weeks to fuse my neck bones together and then after I recover from that they are going to let me get up in a wheelchair and use a neck brace. They don't have much hope that I'll ever regain the use of my arms and legs though. It looks like life as I knew it will be over, forever."

"Not forever, Eliza. When Christ comes again we'll all get new bodies and be whole again."

"Here it comes, you're getting as bad as Jobella! Do you still believe all that nonsense? Look at you you're almost as crippled as I am!"

"Eliza, I have something to tell you. I know you are skeptical about everything, but I need to tell you something. I know you're going to think I'm crazy."

"I already do, but go ahead." I smiled.

"When we were in the wreck, do you remember them telling each other that it was a miracle, that we should have been killed?"

"Go on, tell me what you know."

"Well, when we were about to hit the truck it felt almost like time was suspended. It was then I saw them, Eliza, there were angels all around us! They came between the crushing metal from the front of the car and us. They cushioned us from being killed!"

"That's a lovely story, Billie, but I don't believe that. I think that you were seeing them because you wanted to see them. It was probably your imagination or a hallucination from hitting your head. You don't seriously think that there really are angels that appear to us like that, do you?"

Tears came to Billie's eye then and she wiped them with the tissue she held in her hand.

"I'm sorry, Billie, I wish I could believe your story. Maybe someday I will, but right now I'm too angry to believe in anything, especially in God, and heavenly beings."

"Eliza, I'm going to continue to pray for you. I'm not going to give up on you getting better and believing in God again."

I had to change the subject before she continued. "By the way, I heard that you are going to Jobella's wedding this weekend. Give her my best, will you?"

"I will. I'm happy for her. She deserves this happiness. I just wish her mom and dad could have been there and see her get married." She said and then added, "I love you, Eliza. I do hope you will get well soon. I'll get back to see you when I can."

"You too, Billie. I will think on those things that you told me, I promise. Thank you for your prayers, and I hope you heal soon too, good as new."

Chapter 8

After Billie came in, and interrupted my beautiful dream of running, I tried to settle back down to thinking of nice things from my past again, but my train of thought was destroyed by her ramblings about angels and God. I asked the aide to turn my television on so I could watch something and get my mind centered on something else. Wouldn't you know they would be showing a marathon of 'Touched by an Angel'. "You have got to be kidding me!" I said louder than was necessary.

"You want me to change the channel for you?" asked the aide.

"No, just turn it off. I guess I must not be in the mood for watching anything right now."

"It's time to turn you again, anyway. Is there anything else I can for you?"

"Can you give me my life back?" I joked.

"We're doing our best. If I could, I would!" she smiled.

After she turned me back on my stomach I laid there and tried to think of more pleasant things again, but I couldn't get Billie's angels out of my mind. What if she was right? Was I wrong that I didn't believe in them? Could there have really been angels in that car with us that day? It is strange that none of us were killed. I saw pictures of the wreck. Zoe's SUV was crushed beyond recognition. No one should have survived that.

I was pondering all of these things in my mind, when my Mom, Dad, and Jamie walked in. Actually Jamie ran in. "Liza," he called, "Mom and Dad got you something, but I can't tell you what it is!"

"It's alright Jamie, she's going to find out in a few minutes," Mom told him.

Dad was carrying in what looked like a small desk and Mom had a gift bag and card. Dad came over and set the small desk under my bed under my face. "I just wanted to make sure this would work before we give you your gif,." he said as he set it up. "It looks perfect. Let's try it out!"

Mom brought the gift bag over and first pulled out the get-well card that Dad created. It was an architects rendering of our house. On the cover there was a picture of the outside of our house and on the inside the floor plans. On the back, dad wrote 'For my special princess, Love Dad'.

"I love it Dad, but what does it mean?" I asked.

He put the card on the desk beneath my face, and pointed out a few things to me that I didn't notice on first glance. On the cover of the card he showed me how they were going to put a wheelchair ramp outside the front door so that I would be able come and go in my wheelchair and on the inside, the changes he was going to make to give me a main floor bedroom and bathroom. I started to cry splashing a few tears on the card.

"Well, do you like it?" he asked. "I didn't mean to make you cry."

"It just looks like you are giving up on me getting well. This looks so permanent. Like you don't expect me to leave home after this." I sobbed.

"I didn't mean it that way, honest. We have to face reality. You'll probably need a wheelchair when it's all said and done. We have to be ready. You won't be staying in the hospital forever. If we can't make our home accessible for you, you will have to go to a rehab center or nursing home. I'd rather have you at home, wouldn't you?"

"I guess so, but I'd rather get over all of this. I'm not ready to give up yet. I want to be able to walk and use my hands and arms again."

"That may well happen, but we have to be ready in case it doesn't."

"Mom, you didn't show me what's in the bag yet," I said, changing the subject. If I didn't think about something else, I would start crying.

"Oh, I almost forgot. Look inside!"

"Oh, it's an I-pad! Okay…I love it, but how am I supposed to use it with no fingers?" I asked.

"You'll see!" she laughed. She pulled out a pen with a rubber end to use with it. "We loaded it up with a bunch of books on the Kindle, Nook and I-book apps, and a bunch of games and other apps that we thought you might be interested in using."

"Again, how am I supposed to use it?"

"We spoke with the nurse about how we could make this happen. We figured that the times you had to lie on your stomach, you could have the tablet on the desk under your bed where you could see it and the pen could be in a cup next to the tablet. When you want to use it, you can maneuver the pen into your mouth, and use it to press the icons, or the keyboard." She went on to show me how to use it and then I tried it with my mouth. It took a little work to get the pen to my mouth and then even more work to make it go where I wanted it to go. The first few attempts were disastrous. I kept losing the 'pen', and dropping it on the floor, but after I finally got the hang of it, it was great!

Unfortunately just as I was getting use to it, the aide came in to flip me on my back. They would have to remove my desk and I-pad out from under me every time I had to be turned over. "I wish there was a way we could attached it to the mattress above me so I could continue to use it while I was on my back." I told Dad.

"We'll have to work on that!" he smiled.

The aide said. "We'll see what we can do about letting you get on the Internet here. That would be great for you too. You would be able to go on Facebook and Email to keep up with your friends"

"After your surgery, and when you get in a wheelchair we'll be able to put your desk in front of you and you can use it as an easel." Dad showed me how it could adjust it to different angles. "You might even get where you can draw, paint or even write!"

"Well...between my artistic brother and father, maybe I will. You never know, maybe I inherited your genes too, Dad."

"Thank you both for what you've done. These things will make my days a little less boring. Maybe I can use some of my time actually learning something too, like what's the best way for the 'Angry Birds' to kill those awful pigs!" I laughed.

It actually felt good to laugh again, at least for a little while, but then reality hit again. After Mom, Dad, and Jamie left, I was all alone again. I was on my back and other than watching television there wasn't much more I could do. It's a funny thing about when we have positive experiences in our lives it seems that the lows feel even lower. So again, I fell into a depression, knowing that this would probably be what my life would be for the rest of my life.

The next day was pretty much like the day before and the day before that. I started writing my diary on my tablet on the 'notes' icon.

My first page in my diary went like this:

7:00 am: Nurses bustling at nurse's station. Loud chatter. Change of shift.

7:30: Nurses making rounds. Changing my tube feeding after forcing my meds down my G-tube.

8:00: Aides coming in to give me a bed bath. First my front and then flipped me over and washed my backside.

8:30: Settled down with my I-pad and read for an hour in some random book.

10:00: Aides flipped me to turn me on by back to get ready for therapy. Therapist in to do my range of motion exercises. Highlight of my day, by the way.

11:00: Doctor in to see me. Spends all of five minutes with me discussing everything but my condition. After he leaves I watch "The Price is Right" and "Jeopardy".

12:00: Mom came by with her lunch in hand to visit me on her lunch break. I wonder if she realizes how I hate to see her eat in front of me. What I wouldn't give to be able eat with her. I don't want to hurt her feelings so I don't say anything.

12:30: Mom leaves and aides come in to flip me to my stomach. I get back to reading my book.

2:30: Aides come back to turn me to my back and empty my catheter bag. They talk about what they are going to do tonight after work. Wish I could go with them.

3:00: Shift change, lots of chatter and laughing at some random joke. Wish I was with them working, laughing and having a normal life instead of being in here in bed not being able to do anything.

4:00: Watch "Judge Judy". Get turned to my stomach. Nurse comes in with my afternoon meds and checks out my skin. She freaks out. I'm beginning to get pressure sores along my backbones. Begins skin treatments and puts dressings on them. She calls the doctor to let him know.

5:00: Doctor Anderson comes in again and this time examines my sores. Concerned that they will only get worse because I can't stay on my stomach all the time and laying on my side isn't an option right now. Decides that he will do X-rays in am to see if he can go ahead and move my surgery up.

6:00: Food carts come around. I can smell the food from my room. I don't care if they do say the hospital food is bad. I would give anything to be able to eat something again!

6:30: Dr. wrote the order to keep me on my stomach for two hours and then on my back for only half an hour at a time and keep doing it on that schedule. I don't mind that schedule at all. Gives me more time to read and play games and chat on my tablet.

7:00: Mom and Dad visit. Told them what the doctor and nurses said about my back. Mom was angry. She said that someone wasn't doing their job and had to have left me on my back too long. If they did what they were supposed to do, I shouldn't have gotten them. She said that the aides must not have reported to the nurses that I was starting to have problems.

8:00: Watched television, some procedural crime show. Not too interested but it was something to pass the time.

9:00: Took sleeping medicine and pain pill. Got a terrible headache after my parents left.

That was my usual day, everyday, same thing all the time. I would be glad to get through with my surgery so I could change up my routine.

Chapter 9

The next day they came in to get an X-ray of my neck. I was moved unto my back, and they maneuvered the machine to view my neck from a side angle so they could get a clear image of my spine.

After the doctor read the X-ray he pronounced me healed enough to do surgery, and he set it up for the next day. Finally I would get this over with so I could move on with my life, such as it was, and get out of this horrible bed.

After he left, Eric came by to do my therapy. I let him know that I would be having surgery the next day. He was excited for me that it would finally be done so I could be transferred to a regular room.

"We'll be doing more aggressive therapy when you are finally up in a wheelchair. We'll be able to do a little more with you. We'll take you down to the rehab gym and fit you for braces, and teach you to use your shoulders to control your arms and hands. I may even each you how to write and draw with only your mouth! Later on we'll see about getting you into an electric wheelchair, and train you to use your shoulders to move your hands to control it. You have got a lot to learn before I get done with you!" he said.

"I would rather be able to get up and walk, and use my hands like a normal person, thank you very much!"

"Well, let's just see what happens from here on out. With God anything is possible. You just have to believe!"

"I would rather leave God out of this. If the doctor's can't fix me I doubt that God can. He and I aren't on very good terms right now."

"Well, we can fix that, too!" he smiled. "As long as I'm around being your personal trainer, I'm going to keep reminding you of his goodness."

"As much as I love having you help me, I doubt that even you can move me spiritually."

"We'll see about that," he laughed.

"Do you bug all of your patients about religion?"

"Only the ones I care about and the ones I don't care about!" He smiled.

"What category am I in?"

"What do you think?"

With that he just smiled and walked out the door.

Mom came in her usual time at lunch. I told her what the doctor said about doing my surgery in the morning.

"Well, are you ready for that?"

"I guess I might as well be. It is something that has to be done, right? I'm tired of laying in the bed. I'm eager to at least be getting ready to sit up for a while, even if it is in a wheelchair. I'll be excited to be able to eat real food again as well!"

"You know, I didn't think about that. Does it bother you that I eat my lunch here in front of you?"

"Sometimes, maybe in a few days we'll be able to eat together in my room! That will be nice for a change."

While Mom was visiting me, the nurse came in to have her sign the consent forms for my surgery. The nurse told us about what they were going to do. There was all the scary stuff about how I could die, or develop an infection, or have my spinal cord damaged further, resulting in other system failures. Mom, being a nurse knew that they were required to tell you all of these bad things before you sign so you won't be able to sue if something bad happens. She left after all of the paperwork was taken care of.

That afternoon the anesthetist came by to see me along with the neurosurgeon. They explained to me that they would start an IV and give me some medicine that would help put me to sleep. After I was asleep they would put a tube down my throat and hook me up to a ventilator because, as they said, the anesthesia would paralyze my lungs. They went on to say that I would be on my stomach and they would cut a slit in the back of my neck, and remove any fragments of bone that had broken off, examine my spinal cord to see if they could do anything to repair it, and then fuse together the two damaged vertebrae. After surgery I would go to the recovery room until the anesthesia wears off and I can breath on my own. Then I would be moved to a regular room, in a regular bed with a neck brace instead of this horrible traction. Then I could move on to my next phase of healing!

My Mom, Dad, and Jamie came by that evening after Dad got out of work. I was nervous, but excited about finally going to surgery. Mom and Dad weren't quite as elated as me, but they were anxious to get it over with as well.

They were going to take me the first thing in the morning to surgery and Mom and Dad said that they had both taken the day off so they could stay with me.

"What about Jamie, doesn't he have school?" I asked. Jamie had started school the first week in September. It has been almost two weeks now and from what I heard, he loved it.

"We are leaving him at grandma's again. She will make sure he gets there and will pick him up after school. We will bring him by tomorrow night."

When they left they took my desk and I-pad. They didn't want anything to happen to them after I went to surgery. They would bring them back when I was able to use it again.

I fell asleep and slept most of the night, I was nervous about the surgery, but anxious to get it over with. I fell asleep and dreamt about a time back to my senior year in high school. Billie, Zoe, Jobella and I were sitting in the cafeteria, discussing what we were going to do after we graduated.

"Well the first thing I'm going to do is throw a big party!" I said.

"Are you going to invite all your drinking buddies?" asked Zoe.

"Count me out if you do," Jobella frowned.

"My parent's will be there, so I don't think I'll be able to do much mischief making. I can't help it if some of the guests bring something, though," she smiled.

The night of the party started out a lot of fun. I was sad that Jobella couldn't join us. She was in the hospital following her attack. She probably wouldn't have approved of what happened anyway. Mom and Dad went to dinner and to a movie with Jamie so we could have the evening to ourselves. Mom had made some appetizers, and bought a cake and made some punch for us. I don't think she thought about how easy it would be for someone to spike the punch when she prepared it, and of course, someone did. Before the night was over several of my guests were drunk. They were totally wrecking our house, throwing things around and spilling punch and beer everywhere. I didn't get as drunk as some of them. Zoe and Billie left shortly after the party started when it was obvious that some of my guests were getting out of control. They were getting very uncomfortable with the way everything was going, the rest of my quests were pairing off, and going into the rest of the house to do who knows what. Finally, I knew I had to stop this. It was totally getting weird, even for me. I told everyone to leave so I could get the house straightened up before my mom and dad came home.

After everyone left, I rushed around picking up all the trash and wiping up all the spills. I became worried when the clock rolled around midnight and my family still wasn't home. A few minutes later a patrol car pulled up in our driveway and I heard a knock on the door.

At first I thought that some neighbor had complained about the noise from our party.

"Are you Eliza Goodman?"

"Yes I am. Is something wrong?"

"Are your parent's, Andrew and Sarah Goodman, and do you have a younger brother named Jamie?"

All of a sudden I started to panic. "Yes, has something happened to them?"

"I'm afraid they were in a car accident tonight, about an hour ago. A drunk driver went through a red light a few blocks away from here and hit them. Your family's injuries were all minor. They were treated and released from the hospital and are at the police station now. But the driver that hit them died at the scene when his car flipped over. He didn't have a seat belt on and was thrown from the car. There were three other young people in the car with him. They are at the hospital and are in stable condition. When questioned they said that they had been partying here at your house and had just left."

"Was there drinking here at your home and were you drinking with them?"

"Some of them were drinking, yes, but they brought their own bottles. I had nothing to do with that. My parent's didn't know anything about my guests drinking. We were just celebrating our graduation, you know?"

"We want you to come down to the station with us. If the people in the car are an example of those who were at your party, you and your parents could be arrested for allowing underage drinking and supplying alcohol to minors."

"But my parents and I didn't give it to them. They brought the booze with them. My parent's don't even have any alcohol in the house!"

"We will be returning with a warrant to search your home after we take you in. When we are through, if we find anything, you and your parents will be held pending further investigation. You could just have to pay a fine, and be released, but you all will be in custody at least until we are through searching your house."

When we got to the police station, I ran to my parents and hugged them. I was so glad that they didn't have any major injuries. They were pretty shaken up and had some bruises, but otherwise they were okay. They were very angry with me, however, because I allowed such goings on in our house. They trusted me and I let them down. I wanted to crawl in a hole somewhere. I learned my lesson that night and I never wanted to hurt them again. I told them that some of my school friends had brought their boyfriends with them and they were the ones who had spiked the punch and brought beer. I went on to say that when it was getting out of hand I made everyone leave, but evidently that was when my parents were coming home.

I prayed they wouldn't find any open liquor bottles at the house, but I do remember picking up beer cans and throwing them in the trash can out back. They would be sure to find those. Man, was my life messed up after that incident.

I felt horrible for the guy that was killed and his family. I barely knew him from school so his death didn't affect me all that much. Now that I've been in a horrible wreck, I can sympathize with the other kids that had to go through that accident that killed him, especially his girlfriend. I wasn't responsible for their stupidity of drinking and driving, but I still felt bad for them. I felt worse at the time for my parents. They were innocent of allowing them to drink and here they were getting locked up for something that I allowed to happen and being in a wreck on top of that. I couldn't apologize enough.

I was still asleep and dreaming when they came. "Eliza, wake up honey, it's time to get prepped for surgery." I heard Mom say.

I was still foggy from the bad dream. "Oh, hi, Mom and Dad. Why are you here so early?"

"Did you forget? You'll be going into surgery in a bit. We wanted to make sure we saw you before you go into the OR."

"I'm glad you came. Have I told you lately how much I love and appreciate you?" I said. "You're the best parents in the world and I don't deserve you. I know you've always done what's best for me."

"What brought this on?" Dad asked.

"Nothing, I just wanted to say it, that's all."

"Eliza," the nurse said. "I'm going to start an IV now and give you some medicine that's going to make you sleepy. Then we're going to roll you down to the OR."

That was the last thing I remembered until I woke up in the recovery room.

Chapter 10

"Ms. Goodman, are you awake?" I heard a voice off in a distance. "This is Dr. Anderson, can you hear me?"

I was still kind of out of it. "Yes, sort of. I'm having a hard time waking up."

"That's normal. You will be sleepy most of the rest of the day. I have someone here that wants to say hello."

"Hi princess," I heard my Dad say. "They're getting ready to take you to your room now."

"Hi honey," it was Mom this time. "Welcome back."

"I'm going to talk with all of you when you get settled in your room. I just need to get a little bit of paperwork done and then I'll be up. Briefly I just want you to know that everything went well and about the way we expected it to go. I'll give you more details in a little while."

The operating room recovery aides pushed me up to my room and three of them log rolled me onto a transfer board and slid me into bed. I was a little more awake now. The room was a lot smaller than the room I was in yesterday. I was in a regular bed now with a soft cushiony mattress that's used when they want to prevent further skin breakdown.

Shortly after I was settled. Dr. Anderson came in to talk with us. He talked more to Mom, knowing that she was the nurse in the family and would understand what he was trying to say, and I was too groggy to understand and remember anything.

"The operation was a success from the standpoint of what we were trying to accomplish. There were a few bone fragments that were imbedded next to the spinal cord. We were able to remove the particles that threatened to damage the spinal cord further. We attempted to put the frayed ends of the spinal cord together and put an artificial sheath around it to prevent further fraying of the rest of the cord. We smoothed off the vertebrae and fused the two that were broken together. Since we gave her methylprednisolone when she first came into the ED we were able to prevent further damage to her spinal cord and because of the excellent care of the staff and use of the Stryker frame bed we minimized the extent of damage she could have gotten. The neck bones that were involved were the actually the sixth and seventh cervical vertebrae. That means that she may still have some upper arm movement and feelings. Unfortunately she may never regain use of the fine motor movements in her hands and more than likely she will continue to be paralyzed in her legs. As bad as that sounds, if she had not been treated and not had the surgery she could have lost everything from her neck down including her vital organ functions. In short she could have died. I know you wanted to hear that we were able to repair her spinal cord to where she would be normal again but unfortunately the spinal cord can't repair itself. Scientists are working on some things like electronic stimulating wires and stem cell research, but that is a few years down the road. Right now the best thing for you to do is to accept that she will have to live with the limitations of her paralysis and move forward with her therapy to learn new skills for her life.

"How soon will I be able to sit up and do therapy?" I interrupted.

"Well, we need to let you rest today and maybe tomorrow you can start. You are aware that you are wearing a neck brace now. You will have to wear that until your neck stabilizes where we did your surgery. We took the clamp off your head, so the brace is the only thing keeping your neck vertebrate in place. The staff will be able to logroll you from side to side to keep you off your back, so your pressure sores can heal, but you will have to keep your head and neck in alignment with your back until you are fully healed. They will have to prop your head up with pillows when you are on your side. When you are on your back they can roll the bed up a few degrees a little more each day until you can tolerate a sitting position. Once you do that we can see about you getting in a wheelchair and get you down to therapy. In the meantime they can continue to do your range of motion exercises. Also after you are able to sit up in at least a forty-five degree angle we will begin turning off your tube feedings and try you on some food. If you eat well and can keep it down, we will then remove your feeding tube."

"So talk to me, Eliza, how do you feel about everything I talked about?"

"I am disappointed that the surgery couldn't fix me. I was hoping for some good news, like that I was cured. But deep down inside, I figured that I probably wouldn't get better. I was doing some research on the Internet a few nights ago about spinal cord injuries and I really don't want to be like this the rest of my life. I kind of wish I would've died in that crash. I feel like my life is over anyway."

"Eliza, you shouldn't talk like that!" Mom exclaimed.

"We don't know what we'd do without you, princess. We will figure out a way to make it okay for you." Dad added.

"A lot of people that are paralyzed go on to live good, full lives, Eliza. There have been many cases where the people who have suffered traumatic neck injuries went on and made great contributions to their families and society. There is no reason why you couldn't be one of them." Dr. Anderson said.

"But I'm not one of them. I don't have any talent and I'm not a big name celebrity that has clout with the press to work an agenda."

"Eliza, you have a brain, a heart and a soul. The only difference between you and me, or your friends and family is that you have a body that can't move. We don't think, love, or have internal feelings about things or people with our body. They come from our head and our heart. The sooner you learn that, the sooner you can begin to heal."

"Doctor, all my life I've been very athletic. Running is one of the things that I dearly loved. To think that I'll never be able to do that again is killing me inside."

"We'll I don't know what to say about that. I can give you pat answers to all your concerns, but until you accept that you are no longer that person, you won't be able to move on with your life."

"I suppose you're right. I have a lot to think about. Thank you doctor for trying to help me, and for doing everything you can to fix me up. Will you still continue to check up on me everyday?"

"As long as I'm your doctor, yes I will."

With that he left. Mom and Dad stayed a little while longer. They became unusually quiet as they thought every thing over.

"Dad, I guess you can go ahead with the changes to the house. Thank you for planning it. It's great."

"Mom, thank you for trying so hard to make me more comfortable by staying with me and making sure the nurses do their jobs. I don't say it enough, but I really do appreciate you guys."

"We're going to help you through this, Eliza. We are going to find a way that you can be an inspiration to others. You're life isn't over, I can promise you that." Dad added.

After the doctor spoke to us, they left to go home. They put their arms around my shoulders now that they knew I had feelings in them and kissed my forehead. Somehow the love of my parents and their acceptance of my condition added to my feelings of security and warmth. I could count on them even if I could never depend on anyone else.

After they left, the nurse and aide came in to turn me on my side. It felt strange to get in that position after two months of being flat on my stomach and back. The nurse held my head up as the aide stuffed the pillows under it. Who would have thought that a pillow could feel so good! We really do take an awful lot for granted like being able to touch and feel, such a basic sense, but so powerful. With it we are aware of our surroundings, we caress our loved ones to let them know we care, touch the softness of our pets fur, and feel the firmness of a handshake when meeting someone new. We feel the smoothness of the desk we write on, the warmth of a fireplace on a cool winter day and the coldness of ice as we drop the cubes in our tea on a hot summer day. Yes I would have to learn a whole new way to interact with my surroundings and my loved ones. I just hope I'm up for all the changes I will be going through for the next several months and possibly the rest of my life.

Chapter 11

I was excited when I was finally able to sit up in a wheelchair. Well, as excited as anyone could get in my condition. It was now a week following my surgery. A couple of days ago I ate my first meal. It felt strange, but wonderful, to eat real food after a month of tube feedings. It was still awkward having someone else feed me and give me sips of water. At lunchtime when Mom came to eat with me, she fed me between bites of her own food. It was a unique bonding experience to say the least.

Tonight after midnight they wanted me to not eat anything. They were going to pull out my feeding tube in the morning and they didn't want anything in my stomach.

When the tube was removed they were going to start taking me to the rehab gym to start my intensive training to make me more self-sufficient.

After supper Jobella and Steve came to visit me. It was good to see them again. They had just returned from their honeymoon a few weeks ago and were in school now. I envied them because of their happiness, love, and the ability to get around and do what they liked.

"Hi, how are you doing?" she asked

"A little better, now that I can sit up in a chair."

"So have you gotten anymore results, yet? Are you able to move or feel anything yet?"

"Sometimes I get a little tingling sensation in my fingers. They say that could be a good sign that I'm getting some of my feeling back even if it is annoying. I still can't move anything though." Once in a while I do get a prickly feeling like you feel when your hands get numb and go to sleep.

"How are things emotionally and spiritually for you?" Steve asked.

"I guess I'm doing okay emotionally. I'm starting to get use to the idea that I may never get to use my body again, but those slight feelings in my hands are giving me some hope. I'm going to start therapy the day after tomorrow to do some learning of how to do things with my limitations and they will continue to do range of motion exercises with me and they are going to teach me to do things with my mouth and nose that I never thought I'd use them for. I've learned how to use an I-pad with a stick in my mouth already. Mom and Dad showed me how to do that! Who would of thought?" I smiled. "Dad made a special desk for me that I could use from a wheelchair. Spiritually, I've had a lot of time to think about things laying here in bed for the last eight weeks. I've thought about what you told me and I remember what I told you when you were down. I guess I have head knowledge of God and Jesus but I just don't feel it in my heart yet. I've done a lot of praying, really I have, but they seem to stop at the ceiling. I don't get a response to my prayers, at least not the way you did, Jobella. I'm still angry with God for what's happened to us in the wreck. Maybe I have to let go of that anger and stop blaming God for all of this. Billie came to visit me a few days before your wedding. She was pretty upbeat about everything. She told me about her seeing angels at the crash site. I have a hard time believing that. If angels were there, how come I'm in the shape I'm in, and Zoe is still in and out of a coma?"

"I can only answer this. By looking at the videos and pictures of the car, and the awful shape it was in, all three of you should have been killed. I believe God spared all of you for a reason. I believe he did send his angels to protect you from death. He wanted you to be a believer, Eliza. He wanted you to live so that your life would be redeemed from hell, and to live for him. I can't say whether or not God's purpose is to use you by allowing you to fully recover, or by witnessing from a wheel chair, but I know he wants to be used by you."

"Thank you, Jobella. I'll be thinking on these things. I can pull up the Bible on my I Pad now that Mom brought it back to me along with my 'stick' she got me for my mouth." She smiled. "I can actually read the Bible that way with the Bible app I downloaded."

"Eliza, would you mind if we pray with you before we leave?" Steve asked.

"Sure, why not. I guess I need all the prayers I can get right now."

"Dear Heavenly Father, I pray for Eliza. She is going through a really tough time now. I pray for her recovery, both physically and spiritually, but especially spiritually. We don't always have answers why these things happen to some folks, but not others. We only know that Eliza needs you now. Make her physically sound and help her to recover from her injuries, if it is your will, but we especially pray for your grace to heal her emotionally and spiritually. We know that you can do this and do it well. We don't always have control over our circumstances in life, but we know that you are in control of all things. We lift up our sister, Eliza. Keep her in your arms. Bring her to your saving grace. This I pray in Jesus name, amen"

The prayer brought tears to my eyes. It was the first time that anyone ever said a prayer like that over me.

"Thank you guys. Your visit and your words meant a lot to me. I will start reading my Bible more and praying. I promise."

Mom, Dad, and Jamie came in to see me right after they left. "Hi princess. We passed Jobella and Steven on their way out. Did you have a nice visit with them?"

"I sure did. They are really nice people, I'm glad that they are my friends. Her husband is really nice."

"Did they bring any of their wedding pictures with them?" Mom asked.

"No, I'll have to ask about that the next time I see them. Dad, I see you brought my desk back so I can use it from my wheelchair."

"Yes, we brought it along with your I-pad and some colored pencils and drawing paper for you to practice doing some art work. We can put them in a cup on your over-the-bed table so you can reach them with your mouth."

"Thank you. I'll give it a try. I think they said something about training me to do that type of thing in therapy. This way I'll be able to practice."

The next day after my breakfast and bath, Eric came and got me to take me to therapy. It had been a couple of days since I seen him last. "Good Morning, sunshine! Are you all ready for the next chapter in your life?"

I smiled back at him. "Yes, I think I am, but I warn you. I'm not going to take it laying down!"

"That's the spirit." He laughed.

It felt good getting out of my room and going to the therapy room. I almost felt like I was going to a regular gym with all the equipment I saw there. There were parallel bars, exercise balls, stationary bikes, stair steps, and a series of pulleys, all those things that I couldn't use. Why was I even here?

"We're going to start you out with some range of motion exercises." Eric said. He started putting my arms and legs through their paces, by rotating, flexing, and extending every joint. The only difference from what he had been doing was that I was sitting up now. After that he wanted to start exercising my upper arms and shoulders.

"If we work your shoulders we may be able to develop enough strength in them so that they can lift your lower arms and give you a little leverage in moving your hands. That will be real important when you get ready for your electric wheelchair. You'll be able to use the controls to drive it simply by moving your hands over them."

"Right now we have a special cycle you can use with your arms. I'll fit your hands and forearms with a special brace then attach that brace to the pedals of this arm bicycle. The arm bicycle is attached to the computer. So when you stop pedaling the screen stops. The faster you go, the faster it goes on screen. Your shoulders will do all the moving. While you're 'pedaling' with your hands we will have you watch a moving screen on the computer. You can choose what scenery you want to pedal through on the screen. After you get the hang of going on a 'flat' course we will make it more interesting and difficult for you. We will have you go 'up hill' by tightening the pedals, so you have to push a little harder. Do you think you are ready for that?"

"That actually sounds like fun! Let's do it!" I smiled

He sat me at a table and hooked up arms up like he said. He turned the computer on and a picture of a forest appeared with a dirt pathway. It was hard at first to move the pedals. I lost a lot of strength in my shoulders from not using them for two months. I couldn't believe how weak I was. I started to tear up when I couldn't do it, but Eric was determined that I could. He got behind me and assisted me as I started. It reminded me of when dad was teaching me how to ride a bike. He would hold me until I was steady. Just like Eric was doing now. After we picked up momentum, Eric let go of my shoulders and I started doing it on my own. The forest in the video reminded me of riding a bike or running in a real forest like in my dream. "Now all I need is the wind blowing in my face to complete the experience." I whispered to him.

"We can take care of that!" He said and then went to the office and brought out a small fan.

"You're crazy," I laughed at him, but it really did feel good. I could almost believe I was there and a part of the picture I was seeing on the screen. The computer program even had sound effects. You could hear the birds chirping and the whirring of the bicycle wheels. I was so engrossed with the picture and pedaling through the woods I didn't even think about this being an exercise. I was actually moving my arms myself. Its amazing how little things like moving your shoulders can be so exciting.

It made me sad when my time was up and he had to take me back to my room. "You did awesome today, Eliza."

"Can we do that again? That was actually fun for me. I almost didn't even miss my legs and running."

"We can spend part of the time on that machine every day, but we have some other things we have to do as well. I'm going to have to share you with our other staff. In a week or two we'll be ready to fit you with an electric wheelchair. When we do that you'll have to go through driver's education all over again! Then we're also going to teach you how to get in and out of the chair and bed and on top of that we are going to teach you to be an award winning artist even though I can't even draw a stickman even with two hands!" He smiled.

"You're a real slave driver, aren't you?" I laughed. "I guess there's no rest for the wicked."

"It's all in a days work, m'lady," he bowed. "We're going to make you better than you were before!"

I continued to do well in therapy. Eric was great and my feelings were growing deeper for him with each passing day and I could tell he liked me too. After work each day he would come to see me just to visit. Finally the day came when he said he would like to see me on a social level after I got out of the hospital. He didn't want to be too obvious about our friendship while I was in the hospital though, because his boss wouldn't look too kindly on that. Conflict of interest, he said, and he would probably take him off my case if that happened.

I was basking in my new friendship with Eric and was looking forward to this new phase of my life with him there to love me and help move me forward.

Then it happened...

Chapter 12

"Good Morning Eliza, are you ready for your therapy to-day?" Eric asked, smiling.

"Sure am, I'm more ready just to be with you!" I laughed. "You really give me the incentive to do good so I can get out of here."

We made our way down the hall to the elevators. "It sure is quiet around here this morning," I said. "Where is everybody?"

"They're probably still in bed or eating. We're a little early. I wanted to get some extra time with you today." He bent over and lightly kissed the top of my head and squeezed my shoulders.

"Do they know at the nurse's station that I left early?" I asked.

"I'm not sure, but they should be aware by this time that I come to get you early so we can have more time in the therapy gym to get you ready to get out of here."

"So you're trying to get rid of me, huh?" I smiled.

"I just want you to be able to have a real life again. Don't worry, you know I'm not going anywhere! I could even schedule some off duty therapy with you at your house, if you want." He smiled back at me and squeezed my shoulder again.

I heard the familiar ring of the elevator signal. As we got on the elevator, we felt a slight bump. I started getting a little worried. I never felt the elevator do that before.

"What was that?"

"I'm sure it was nothing, elevators do that sometimes. We might have felt the vibration from the elevator next to us."

Then within seconds, there was a second vibration slightly larger than the first.

"I'm really getting concerned about it now. Can we get off at the next floor?"

"If you're that worried, sure."

Before we could reach the next floor, there was a very large jolt, and the whole elevator was shaking. Then the lights went out, and we were in total darkness. Even the emergency lights didn't come on. I felt something fall against my chair. Then I heard a very large boom and it sounded like the ceiling was caving in. I was afraid that the whole elevator was going to fall.

"Eric, I'm scared!" I cried out. "I'm really scared now!"

He didn't answer.

"Eric, where are you?"

There was still no answer.

"Eric, this isn't funny, answer me now!"

Nothing.

I started screaming for help. I yelled louder than I ever yelled before. I kept on until my voice threatened to give out.

Something was wrong with Eric. He wouldn't answer me. It was so dark I couldn't see anything. He must have been knocked out by something.

"God, if you can see me in this darkness and hear me, please answer my prayer. Please let Eric be all right and save him, save us. I'm so afraid right now. God, I know that I've not been everything you've wanted me to be my whole life and I'm sorry. Please forgive me. Here in this darkness I'm so alone and afraid. I don't know what's wrong with my friend. He needs you. He's not done anything wrong and he loves you. Please let him be okay. As for me God, I've always been in trouble for one reason or another and I deserve this, but he doesn't. In this situation I'm in right now, I realize that when everything else is gone, the only thing that remains is you and I. God, in this dark elevator I want to turn my life over to you, every bit of it. Not just for today, but for always. I'm not asking this because I fear for my life and for the life of my friend, but suddenly I realize I'm tired of running away from you. Lord, I want Jesus to come into my life and save me. In his name I pray, amen"

In the darkness of the elevator when I finished praying I felt a little lighter, kind of like all my burdens were lifted off my shoulders. I felt totally at peace even though I was in danger of losing what was left of my life.

I could hear some more rumblings around me and I thought that I heard some muffled voices from outside the elevators. I didn't know where it was coming from. It still felt like the earth was shifting. Even though I couldn't feel anything through my body, I could sense it through my shoulders and neck.

I don't know how long we were in there, but I know that the air supply was getting limited. I started to feel faint because I wasn't getting enough oxygen. I started gasping for air. If someone didn't find us soon, we would be both dead.

I know that elevators have emergency call buttons and phones, but I couldn't reach them and who knows where they were anyway, even if I could move, I wouldn't know where to look. How I wish I could do even that simple thing.

"Eric, please wake up, I pleaded again. Eric, I need you! We can't get out. Nobody knows we're here."

There was still no answer.

"Help! Anybody out there?" I yelled again. I didn't want to yell too much because it would take more oxygen to scream like that.

I finally gave up and let sleep overtake me. When I woke up I was in a daze, I thought I heard something outside of the elevator.

Maybe maintenance men and other emergency workers were trying to get to us. I prayed that this was so.

I was too tired to yell anymore. I definitely could hear voices outside the elevator now. They were getting closer to us. Finally I saw a sliver of light coming through the doors. It was so bright after being in the darkness for so long. I started wondering if I had died and this was the 'proverbial light at the end of the tunnel'. As they opened the door wider and my eyes adjusted, I looked around. Eric was lying on his side covered in debris. I could see that he had a head wound and that he was bleeding. He evidently had been knocked unconscious. He was still out of it when the medics took him out on a stretcher. They checked for a pulse real quick and thankfully he was still alive. After he had been taken out, they came back after me and lifted my wheelchair with me in it out of the rubble and took me to a triage area.

"How did you know that we were in the elevator?" I asked.

"Someone at the nurse's station down the hall said that they heard the emergency buzzer go off and they called us."

"How did they hear the buzzer? Eric was knocked out the whole time and I couldn't get to it because I am paralyzed. Does it go off automatically when the elevator shuts down?"

"No, someone has to push it," he responded. "I don't know how it happened, but it's a good thing that it was pressed, because if it were any later, we wouldn't have pulled either of you out alive. The oxygen level in there was near zero. You must be doing something right. Someone is watching over you!"

As I was being pulled out of the elevator, I looked around me. There was rubble everywhere and there were emergency workers, firemen, and police throughout the area. The nursing staff was running around checking on patients and moving some of them around.

I was startled at what I saw. "What happened?"

One of the firemen told me that we had an earthquake. It was very unusual for our area. "I thought that only happened on the west coast!"

"It wasn't a very large one, but when they built the hospital they didn't think about earthquakes and didn't build it up to earthquake codes so even this size earthquake did a lot of structural damage." He replied.

"What are they going to do with all the patients?" I asked, worrying about Eric and Zoe especially.

"They are moving the more serious patients out to other hospitals in the area. Some of them are going to be released early to their homes and some that are needing more therapy and aren't quite ready to be sent home will be sent to nursing homes to finish their therapy."

As I looked around the unit, I didn't recognize anyone. I wasn't on my 'home' floor. No one knew me and how to get in touch with my family, no one even asked. They were too busy with their own patients, and getting them situated to care what happened to me.

They somehow were finally able to restore the power in the building. Hospitals were always a priority for the electric company due to the life saving equipment powered by electricity. The generator had a limited amount of power for emergencies, but it wasn't enough to power the whole hospital.

They wouldn't let anyone up or down in the elevators, of course, because of the damage in the shafts. They couldn't chance anyone being stuck in them in case of aftershocks.

So I waited. After about three hours someone finally came over to me, asked my name, what unit I was on, and who I wanted notified.

When I told them I was from the intermediate care unit, they called the nurse to let her know I was down there. A few minutes later she came down with a couple of men that was helping out on her unit. Because of the elevator being down they had to manually bring me in my wheelchair up the stairs. It was a frightening experience to be carried that way. I was afraid they were going to drop me, or jar my neck causing more damage. I prayed that they knew what they were doing!

It was comforting being back on my unit with the nursing staff that cared for me and knew my condition. There was damage on that unit as well, and the staff was racing around trying to determine what the next steps were in figuring out where we were all going to go. Most of the patients on that unit would probably go to nursing homes because a lot of us were having long term rehab.

They called my Mom and Dad to let them know that I would be moving to a nursing and rehab facility before the day was over.

Chapter 13

Sunnyside Woods was a nursing and convalescent center on the north side of Clairmonte. It was about fifteen miles from our home. As the ambulance that I was in, pulled up to the facility, I was pleasantly surprised at how pretty it was on the outside. It was surrounded by lovely gardens and the front lobby was inviting. It seemed nice enough on first impressions.

Mom and Dad met me there to help me get settled in. I was put in a private room per my parent's request and I was happy with that decision. Going back to my room, I noticed that most of the resident's were elderly that lived here. Not that I had anything against the older generation, but I didn't think that I could relate to them on too many levels. I've never been around elderly people. Even my grandparents were living in another part of the country and I barely ever saw them.

"I don't want to have to stay here too long, this is a place people go to while they are waiting to die, or having to live for a long time because they can't help themselves," I whispered to Dad. "Do you think you'll have our house finished before long?"

"I didn't want to have to tell you this," he began, "but we had some damage to our house as well. We're going to need some work done on it to stabilize the structure before we can even think about building the additions on it like we talked about."

"How long do you think it will take?"

"It's hard to know right now. It seems like all the contractors in the area are working on the major buildings like the hospital first. It will be a while before they can start on residential homes."

"Can't you do anything yourself? You're an architect for goodness sake."

"I'm a pencil pusher, not a contractor or builder. I leave the heavy stuff to others."

"You need to have more therapy anyway. They didn't finish what you needed at the hospital and you're still not even in an electrical wheelchair yet. You have to have more therapy done before you're ready to come home." Mom added.

"Well, you're a nurse, can't you take care of me?"

"I'm a nurse, not a therapist. I can't give you what you need and you know I have to work. I can't take time off now. We're going to need a lot of extra money for your care. Nursing homes aren't cheap and our insurance isn't going to cover the whole cost of you staying here. If I quit my job now, I would lose what insurance we do have. Besides, who would take care of your basic needs while I'm at work?"

"I guess you're right. I didn't think about all that. Can you at least bring me some things from home, so that we can fix this room up a little? Sunnyside Woods may have a cute name and a pretty exterior, but the rooms leave a lot to be desired. It is really plain looking with its ugly aged and yellowed wallpaper and what's up with only having blinds at the windows. Can we at least get some curtains and pictures for the room?"

Mom smiled. "I think we can take care of some of that. Let's see what we can do."

After they left my nurse and aide came into my room.

"Hi, I'm Alex, I'm going to be your nurse until seven tonight and this is Samantha, your nursing assistant."

"You can call me, Sam." She smiled.

"We've gotten your paperwork from the hospital and saw that you were in a really horrible accident and broke your neck, is that right?" asked Alex.

"Yes and I was suppose to continue getting therapy at the hospital until the earthquake hit, and they had to evacuate everyone to other facilities."

"We've gotten a few of the patients earlier today. It filled us up. I believe you got our last bed!"

"Did you get any younger patients like myself in the transfers?"

"We have a few young ones but they've been here for a while. We can't really talk about those, but I'm sure you'll meet some of them in therapy and other group activities." Alex added.

"I can't do anything for myself right now. They were starting on some things with me in therapy, but didn't get too far. I can't move anything below my shoulders, but they were working on that, and I can't maneuver in my wheelchair at all."

"Don't worry," Sam said. "We'll be careful with you and help you do everything. I'm sorry that you had to leave the hospital just as you were making some progress. I'm going to take you on a little tour of our place. Maybe we can see some of the others that are close to your age. If we do, I'll introduce you to them."

"That sounds good, but it's not like I'll be able to go visit them, but maybe some can come see me."

Sam took me for a tour of the whole building. There had to be at least a hundred rooms. Most of them were semiprivate with two residents in each. I was thankful for having a room to myself when I saw how crowded they were.

I met a couple of other girls that were about my age. One had muscular dystrophy and the other multiple sclerosis. They both were coherent, alert and orientated and were also in wheelchairs same as me but unlike me they did have some limited mobility, and were able to scoot around. I told them my room number and invited them to come visit me sometime.

After our introductions, Sam showed me where the dining room was. It was large and had several tables with tablecloths and floral centerpieces and room for wheelchairs to maneuver between the tables. It had pretty floral wallpaper and several pieces of framed artwork on the walls. The windows had curtains that matched the tablecloths. From the ceiling hung chandeliers. If you didn't know you were in a nursing home, you'd think that you were in a really nice restaurant. I looked forward to eating there at meal times instead of my room. I hoped the food was good.

"The dining room is really nice," I commented to Sam.

"Yes, we are really proud of it. Meals are served buffet style. When we bring you in here to eat we will push you through the serving line and you will be able to choose what you want. We'll of course, plate it for you and bring it to your table to feed you. They actually have pretty good food here. I think it's much better than the hospital.

Also we have large activities in here as well, like our worship services. Are you interested in going to the church services?"

"I sure am. I came to know the Lord personally at the hospital and I'm looking forward to growing in him and worshipping with others."

"That's great. I'm a Christian as well. I don't know where I'd be without him."

We went down to the gym. It looked very similar to the therapy department at the hospital, but the clients were different.

There was a group of the elderly residents tossing a beach ball back and forth. In the hall outside of the gym another resident was learning how to steer her electric wheelchair by going in and out of 'traffic cones' placed about six feet apart. "Will I have to do that when I get an electric wheelchair?"

Sam laughed. "You sure will. It's like driver's education all over again. Do you know when you'll get your chair yet?"

"I haven't heard anything. I think they want me to be able to use my hands a little before that."

"Our therapists are really good here. They'll work with you and help you get where you need to be."

"I'm going to miss my therapist that worked with me at the hospital though, he was great. He had me do this pedaling thing with my hands and actually got my shoulders working where I could move my lower arms and hands."

"Maybe our therapist can contact him and get ideas for continuing what he started. We actually have a computer program that you can do the pedaling thing with as well. It might be the same thing."

"You probably won't be able to get in touch with him anytime soon. I was actually in the elevator with him going to therapy when the earthquake hit and he was hurt real bad when part of the elevator ceiling fell on his head. He was knocked unconscious and had to be taken somewhere on a stretcher. I don't know where he is now." I started to cry then.

"You really cared for him didn't you? I know a lot of patients get close to those who take care of them like doctors, nurses and therapists."

"This was more than that kind of relationship. We were actually going to start dating when I got out of the hospital."

"Oh, wow, that is rough. I'm so sorry. I hope you find out where he is and how he's doing."

"Me too. Will you remember us in your prayers? I would really appreciate that."

"Sure, no problem. Well I guess we'd better get you back to your room. The nurse will think we got lost!"

When we got back to my room my parent's had returned and brought a few things with them to set up my room. They brought my favorite quilt from my bedroom and my favorite stuffed animal. It looked like a real curled up cat. It was almost the same color of my cat, Snickers. The stuffed cat had soft fur and it would purr if you pressed on it in just the right spot. It would feel good up against my face and shoulder. They made sure the 'purr' button was close to my face.

They also brought my desk that Dad had made, and of course my I-pad, a sketchbook, and some colored pencils. There was already a television in the room and so they placed the remote where I could reach it with my I-pad pen, and I could press the buttons with that. It actually worked out pretty good as long as I didn't drop it. They set up my cup with my drawing supplies next to my I-pad and drawing tablet.

The biggest surprise was a picture that my mother found in the hospital gift shop. It was a picture of Jesus kneeling beside a woman in a wheelchair. He was laying his hands on her arms and praying with her. It was so beautiful. Jesus looked loving and compassionate towards her. There was a kind of glow around the person in the chair and she was attempting to stand. Behind Jesus and the woman in the wheelchair, there were angels lifting her up. She had such a beautiful smile on her face. The picture was perfect! If I could've hugged my mom I would've. I would just have to be content to have her hug me and I kissed her cheek when she did. I came to love that picture and every time I felt down I would look at it and say a prayer and it would lift me back up emotionally every time.

After they left for home, Sam came and got me ready for supper.

"Wow, they really fixed your room up. It looks more lived in now." Then she saw the picture on my wall. "That painting is amazing! I've never seen one like it before!"

"Mom said she got it at the hospital gift shop. I love it too. It's so inspirational."

"Tell me about this desk set up in the corner."

"Well Dad made the desk especially for me. When I'm up in my wheelchair it can be angled like an easel. It has a side that stays horizontal to hold my pencils and my stick for my I-pad. And the easel side has a ledge so that my I-pad or sketchbook doesn't slide off. I can go on my I-pad or draw with my mouth. Well I'm not real great with the drawing yet but I'm learning."

"That is so cool! Later when we're not so busy I'd love to have you show me the way you do all that. Right now we'd better get going to the dining room for supper before it all gets cold."

When we were in the dining room I went through the serving line with Sam. I saw my two new 'friends' and asked if I could sit with them.

Sam concentrated on feeding me while the other two girls were able to feed themselves with special eating utensils. Sam put a special extra long curved straw in my iced tea and positioned it so I could sip on it without her assistance.

I learned my friends names while we were in the dining room eating supper and I learned a little bit more about them. The one with muscular dystrophy was named Akeylia Simmons and the one with multiple sclerosis was Katelyn Gray. I didn't want to ask them about their conditions but I thought that I would look at those two conditions on the Internet when I got back to my room.

I did find out that they would be interested in visiting with me in my room and wanted to include me in their friendship. We made a date for them to come the next day after lunch.

Akeylia told me that she had what is called limb-girdle muscular dystrophy. I looked it up and found out that it mostly affected the hips and shoulders. The symptoms I saw on line were muscular weakness, pain, contractures, and possible cardiac, and respiratory problems from the muscles in the chest being compromised. The muscle weakness was progressive and she would probably need to continue to use a wheelchair the rest of her life. The article went on to say that they can live a normal life span, but they could die young due to heart or lung problems. Physical therapy is the primary treatment for this and was essential to remain mobile as long as possible.

Katelyn's multiple sclerosis is an autoimmune disorder that affects the central nervous system. The MS website said that it affected the nerves in that it destroyed the myelin sheath that protects them and when scarring happens it can block the nerve impulses to the muscles and other body parts. The person struggling with MS has fatigue, numbness and tingling sensations, problems with balance and walking, not to mention depression, poor muscle coordination and weakness in the arms and legs. They are usually treated with medications but exercise and therapy are important to maintain muscle strength.

When I read about what they were going through, I almost forgot about my own problems. They were almost as crippled as I was but their conditions could be life threatening, and would only get worse not to mention they were probably in pain on most days.

Understanding what they were going through would help me to get to know them on a more personal level. I believe I could develop real friendships with them, maybe even on a spiritual level. Maybe there was a reason that I was brought to this place at this time.

Chapter 14

Eric woke up in the ICU of a different hospital two days after he suffered from a head injury during the earthquake that caused so much damage at the hospital in Clairmonte. He slowly reached up and touched his head. He felt the gauze that was wrapped around his head and he could feel the bruising around his eyes.

"Where am I?" He asked. "I don't recognize this place. What happened to me?"

"You suffered a major concussion when chunks of the ceiling fell on your head during the earthquake the other day. You were transferred to our hospital because of the damage to the ICU at Clairmonte. You had some fluid built up in your brain and the doctor had to drain it." replied his nurse.

"I don't remember anything. I can't even remember my name or what I do."

"Your name is Eric Evans. You are a physical therapist at Clairmonte Memorial Hospital. Do you know what day this is?"

"I'm not sure. How long have I been here? I wish I could remember something…everything is a blank. "

"You've been unconscious for two days. The doctor said that you could have some memory loss because the bruising was on the frontal part of the brain, the part that regulates your memory. He thinks that as the swelling and bruising subside that you'll get most, if not all, of it back."

"I hope so, I feel like I'm in a brain fog. This is really uncomfortable. I can't even remember what I was doing when I was hit. I just remember everything going black."

"After you recuperate and your family takes you home, maybe they can take you by the hospital to the therapy department and some other familiar places. That will usually bring back some of the memories. Eventually you'll piece everything together and then you should be able to go back to functioning as you did before."

"Let's hope so, because right now I don't even remember being a therapist, let alone what I do in that job."

The doctor came in a few minutes later to talk with him after he found out that he was awake.

"Welcome back to the world, Mr. Evans." The doctor smiled. "The nurse tells me you can't remember anything that happened. Let me tell you what I know and see if it sparks anything for you. Sometimes visual cues and facts from the incident can bring your memory back in bits and pieces."

"Okay, if you think it will help. Anything to bring it back because it is very uncomfortable not remembering anything."

"You were starting your day as a physical therapist at Clairmonte Memorial Hospital two and a half days ago. It was eight o'clock in the morning on September thirtieth. You were pushing a patient down to therapy in an elevator. The earthquake hit right after you got in the elevator and the ceiling caved in on you. Pieces of the ceiling hit your head causing your concussion and it resulted in you becoming unconscious. The electricity had gone out in the hospital and for a couple of hours you and the patient were trapped in the elevator. She couldn't ring the emergency alarm because of being paralyzed and no one knew you were in there. By the time you were rescued the oxygen levels fell so low it's surprising that you both weren't dead when they found you. They eventually brought you here to our hospital, and they took the young lady to a nursing home because the hospital had to be evacuated."

"What was the young lady's name again and is she going to be alright?"

"They didn't tell me her name. I do know she was very sleepy from the low oxygen levels but from what I understand she didn't have any physical injuries from the debris. However, they did tell me that she was visibly upset over you getting injured. Like I said, she had to be moved to a nursing and rehab center, but I'm not exactly sure where she was taken. After you get out of here and get your memory back, you may want to try and contact her to let her know you're alright."

"I'll be sure to do that."

"We'll probably keep you a few more days until you get some of your memory back, we do a follow-up MRI to make sure there is no further bleeding and inflammation around your brain and make sure you are stabilized enough to go home. Your parents told me you could stay at their home until you regain more of your memory and are able to return to work and live on your own again. You'll probably need assistance for a little while and you should be out of work for at least a month. Maybe by then, Clairmonte Memorial will be reopened for patients."

After lunch Eric tried to take a nap. He was aware of all of the monitors and alarm signals going off around him, and the busy nurses and aides running around tending all of the other patients. They were busier than usual because of the extra patient load due to the transfers from Clairmonte. They gave Eric a sedative to help him rest and block out the commotion surrounding him. They felt he needed to relax to help his brain heal.

That afternoon the constant sounds of the unit stimulated flashes of memories. He remembered being around hospital personnel and working in a hospital setting. He remembered assisting patients, but he just couldn't remember exactly what his job was.

That evening when his parents came in they brought in photographs of family members and his dog, Toby. He had always been close to his golden retriever. They hoped by showing him the pictures, he would remember the pet he loved and then remember them in association with his dog. The nurse who called them said to bring in photographs when they come in. She thought it would be helpful to jog his memory.

"Hi Eric," said his Mom as she walked through the door with his Dad, "how are you doing?"

Eric sat straight up in the bed. "Who are you and who is that man with you?"

"Eric, we're your mom and dad, don't you even recognize us?" frowned his mother. It was worse than she thought.

"You look familiar, but I can't quite place where I've seen you before. Man, I'm really messed up aren't I?"

"That's alright, son, it will all come back to you. We brought some pictures to show you, maybe they will help." His dad added.

"I'll try, but it maybe too soon. I may have to wait a few days before everything starts to gel for me. Maybe after I go home, and am in familiar surroundings, it will come back more. Don't give up on me, okay?"

"Well, all we can do is try. We would never give up on you. We will love you always, at least remember that!"

As Eric looked at the pictures of his house and his family, including his younger brother David and sister Lisa, he continued to look puzzled. Then he saw a picture of Toby. "That's my dog! I recognize him. That's Toby!"

His parents had gotten Toby as a month old golden retriever for him when he was a teenager. They were concerned that he was pulling away from their family, and not caring for anything when he was about fifteen years old, so they got him the puppy thinking that the responsibility of caring for a pet would help him learn to care more for others. He had loved Toby with a love he'd not felt for a very long time. After Toby had grown, the dog had started taking on the characteristics of the retriever in him and started chasing cars and bicycles down the street. It was at that time, when one of the neighbors was backing out of their driveway, and not seeing Toby, backed over him. Eric had seen the accident and was inconsolable when he saw that his dog had two broken hind legs. He nursed him back to health and helped him learn to walk again. His parents swore that this was when the desire to become a physical therapist hit him. Toby's miraculous recovery could only be contributed to the care Eric had given him.

"Where's Toby now?" he asked. "Who's taking care of him while I'm here?"

"It's alright, son, he's at our house. Trust me, your brother David isn't letting him out of his sight. He's getting every bit of the loving that you would've given him."

"That's good, I can't wait to see him again."

He continued looking at the pictures, hoping that something else would continue to stir some memories. He asked if they would leave the photos, so he could look at them again later.

The next day they moved him to a regular room. He was out of danger now and didn't need as much monitoring. They thought he'd be able to rest better and get back doing routine activities of daily living in a regular room. By doing as much as he could by himself would help his recovery.

Later that afternoon, his parent's came by and brought some current magazines they knew he liked, his Bible, and one of the devotional books he enjoyed reading. They also showed him a recent newspaper that told about the earthquake and the damage to the hospital where he worked.

Eric had spent a lot of time reading his Bible and had a lot of notes where he studied it in depth. Religion was important to him, so having his Bible and devotional study book would help him in rediscovering who he was. He read over some of the notes he made while he was still in college.

The notes brought him back in time four years earlier. After Eric left to go to college, he had become involved with the wrong crowd, as so many do when they taste freedom for the first time away from the restrictions of home. He was in sports and played football during his first two years. He was toying with what major he wanted to go into and finally settled on sports medicine and physical therapy. He had normally made good grades in all his classes, but when he started hanging out with some of his football friends, his grades started to slide. After failing a few classes his sophomore year, they threatened to kick him out of the program and were threatening him with dismissal from school because he was there on a football scholarship.

Then he met Angela. She was in his anatomy and physiology class. He was having difficulty with the class and she offered to help him study and work as his lab partner. As the semester progressed they became closer and started dating. He didn't realize it until they went out on their first date that she was different than the others he had dated. She didn't believe in going to bars and other questionable places he was used to going to. He found out that she was a Christian and her idea of a great date was meeting with her friends at the local Youth for Christ meeting and then going to one of their favorite hang-outs after it was over.

He liked Angela very much, so he decided that he'd humor her and go to one of her meetings. What he didn't expect was that he would enjoy it so much. That night was the beginning of the new direction in his life.

The guest speaker that night was a former football star at the school. He related to the group about how he had everything going for him and how he was supposed to be drafted by one of the NFL teams. Before the draft he was going out with the guys to celebrate, had too much to drink, and had taken some drugs beside the alcohol. He thought he could handle it when he drove himself and some friends around looking for another bar. They were speeding down the highway on their way across town and got in a serious accident. His best friend was killed and his girlfriend was severely injured. He didn't know it at the time, but she was pregnant with his baby and she lost it in the wreck.

After the accident he was inconsolable. He continued drinking and doing drugs until he lost everything else. He didn't have a job and was no longer being considered for the pros, his girlfriend left him, he embarrassed his family, and they disowned him. He was living on the streets and in homeless shelters, when he could get in one and when he couldn't find a meal at the shelter he went through trashcans outside of restaurants and bars. He even managed to find tossed away alcohol bottles that still had some drink left in them.

One night he had gotten into a fight with one of the other men living at the shelter. He had pulled a knife on him and the other man grabbed it and stabbed him. The pastor at the shelter took him to the hospital and stayed with him until he was well enough to leave. Then he took him into his own home and tried to rehabilitate him. While he was there, he stole some of his wife's jewelry and pawned it to get some money for drugs. When the pastor found out about what he had done, he thought that he would surely throw him back on the streets. He was surprised when the pastor prayed for him and forgave him. After that incident, he allowed him to continue to stay in his home and the preacher worked with him until he was clean from the drugs. It was a difficult time for both of them, especially while he was going through withdrawal.

Tears came to his eyes as he continued with his story telling about how the example and caring of the pastor helped him to re-evaluate his life, and he learned about the love of God and his forgiveness. He learned about Christ and what he had to go through to forgive the sins of people just like him. Because of the compassion of the pastor, who cared for him, he decided to become a Christian, and then went back to school to become a preacher. Now, his ministry was to work with the same type of people that he use to hang out with. After his life turned around, he started going around the country to different schools to tell his story, hoping to prevent others from going down the same road that nearly cost him his life.

After the meeting Eric stayed around and talked with him. He saw a lot of himself in the speaker and became worried that he could end up the same way if he wasn't careful. The pastor prayed with him, and talked with him some more about how to become a Christian and how Christ could turn his life around if he was willing.

Eric became a Christian that very night. He gave his life to Christ and begged him for forgiveness. Since that night his life did turn around and he never went back to the reckless and sinful life he was living. He remained friends with Angela while they were in college, but after she graduated, he lost track of her. The last he heard, she had moved to Montana and was a nurse somewhere over there. Maybe she was what her name implied, maybe she was an angel and that's all she would ever be to him.

After that night, he joined a local church and became active in the youth ministry and worked especially with disadvantaged and handicapped kids.

When he turned his life around, he started acing all his classes and graduated with his master's degree in physical therapy a year early.

He was amazed that he could remember an incident that happened over four years ago in school, but he couldn't remember four days ago. He remembered a girl named Angela from his distant pass that he hadn't seen for three years, but he couldn't even remember the name of the girl that he was taking care of the day the earthquake hit and robbed him of his memory, the one that was trapped with him in that elevator.

Chapter 15

The therapy aide came to get me soon after breakfast. I was anxious to get to my therapy and asked them if they could start with me early. They were going to start working with my shoulder muscles again. This would be the first time since I left the hospital to do these exercises. I was hoping they had the same type of equipment that the hospital had used with me. I actually enjoyed the pedaling exercise that Eric helped me with.

The aide started me out by doing my range of motion exercises. She did my rotations at the shoulder level, then moved down my arm and exercised my full arms. Then she started working my lower arms and hands. When they finished with my arms, she and another aide moved me to the exercise table and while I was laying flat on the exercise bed, she worked my legs, knees, and feet.

As she was moving my shoulders and arms, I could feel the tingling in my hands again. It was more pronounced then it was before and it caused me to continue to hope that I may still have a chance to get at least some feeling and movement back in my hands.

After they moved me back to the wheelchair, they started warming up my shoulders again. They put the braces on my lower arms and connected me to the computer cycling program. It was the same one I had used at the hospital and I was excited that I was going to be able to use it here as well. It definitely wouldn't be as much fun as when Eric did it with me, but I still enjoyed it.

They tried to get me to raise my hands by using my shoulder muscles. It was really hard, and the first several times I tried, I just couldn't do it. When the therapist saw how frustrated and discouraged I was getting, she pushed down on my shoulder and told me to try and push against her hand. When I did that I was amazed that my hand came up about an inch off the armrest of my chair!

"Did you see that?" I cried.

"See, you can do it! You just have to remember to use your shoulder to move your hand. Eventually you'll be able to lift your arm higher and higher and move it from side to side to move your hands in different directions. After enough practice, you'll be able to graduate to an electric wheelchair and then your world will change for the better. Soon you'll be able to get around more and pretty much go wherever you want to!"

"That sounds great! At least it's something I can look forward to."

After therapy and lunch was over, I settled back in my room. I decided to try and do some drawings while I waited on Akeylia and Katelyn.

The sketchpad was opened to a blank sheet of paper and my cup with my pencils was close by. Dad put a piece of tape around the top of each pencil. It not only showed the color but it gave me something to help me grip the pencil in my teeth. I could choose the color I wanted and then pick it up with my mouth. It was awkward at first when I tried to use them, and I would drop the pencil occasionally, but once I got the hang of holding it with my back teeth it started getting easier and I was able to control them better. I started out with basic shapes and doodling. Someday, I would laugh at all these silly drawings that looked like a toddler drew them. I tried writing my name as well, but again it looked like a child's handwriting. Maybe one day it will look right, but it would take a lot of practice for me.

As I was finishing my 'masterpieces', Akeylia and Katelyn rolled into my room.

"Welcome to my room. I missed you two at lunch!"

"We have to eat at a different time than you because we don't need assistance with eating and you have to have someone help you. We hate it, because we would really like to eat with you." Katelyn said.

"I ate with you last night. What was the difference then?"

"I think it was because you were new and they hadn't scheduled you yet." Added Akeylia.

"I guess that would explain why I was the only one in the room that they were feeding." I smiled.

"Wow, that picture is gorgeous!" said Katelyn when she saw my painting on the wall.

"My Mom bought it for me and brought it here when they were setting up my room. I really like it too."

Akeylia added, "wouldn't it be nice if that was true? If all we had to do was say a prayer and Jesus and his angels would come and magically raise us out of these awful wheelchairs and let us walk again?"

"I believe if we have faith enough, God can do anything. If it wasn't so, than we're all doomed. What would we have to live for, if not for hope?" Replied Katelyn.

"You two can live in your fantasy world if you want to. I'm not going to hope for anything. I was made this way and that's all there is to it. It's in my genes and I'll just have to deal with it.

This is my reality, not some pie in the sky cure waiting for me. I mean, if there is a God why would he let the three of us suffer like this. We should be out living life, enjoying it, and meeting and marrying some guy, and have a house full of kids, not stuck here in a nursing home with all the other residents. No offense to all the elderly, but the three of us are the only ones our age here. Everyone here is older and can't even get out of their beds without assistance. It's so pathetic!" Akeylia sighed.

"I had no idea you felt this way, Akeylia. Here we've been here together for over a year and I didn't know you didn't believe in God. You've been going to the worship services on Sundays and the other activities, like when the church choirs come in." Katelyn replied.

"So what else is there to do around here? That is our only social life. It gets me out of my room a few times a week. My family hardly ever even comes in to see me anymore. I think they feel guilty or something. They know this is an inherited condition and they feel it's all their fault." Akeylia responded.

"I'm so sorry you feel this way too, Akeylia. I don't know what to say. I haven't been a Christian very long myself, and like you, I had a head knowledge, but until I had my own conversion experience, I didn't understand what it was all about. I fought against it as well, but when it really comes down to it, when it gets down to just you and no one else, that's when God does his best work. You have to let go of your anger over your circumstances, give it to God, and then he can start making it better."

"Eliza, would you mind if we started a Bible study together?" Katelyn asked me. "It looks like a great way to support each other. I've actually been a Christian for several years and you are new to the faith. If Akeylia wants to come and be a part of it too, that would be great! How about it, Akeylia?"

"I guess so, if I don't, I'll lose my best friend and the possibility of getting another new friend." Akeylia replied. "I guess it can't hurt anything."

"That's the spirit!" I laughed. "Maybe after we get studying more, I can have my friend's husband come in and talk with us. He is in school now to be a preacher and because of some of the things that he and Jobella shared with me about God, is part of the reason that I became saved. They actually had their own trials over the past year. He was in a coma for six months and he had to relearn how to walk again as well. They helped me realize that there was still something I could do, even in this wheelchair."

Katelyn was excited about the Bible study and getting together everyday. We made a secret pact that we were going to diligently pray for Akeylia and lift her up to God.

That evening, my Mom, Dad, and Jamie came by to see me. I told them about my new friends and our plans to do a Bible study. They thought that it was a wonderful idea. They were excited when I told them I accepted Christ while I was in the hospital. They said they have been praying for my salvation a long time. Sometimes, God has to literally knock you flat on your back to get your attention. I know he did me.

I showed them my doodling sketches. I know they wanted to laugh at them and had to hide their smiles. "It's okay you can smile at them. One of these days I'm going to be famous and these scratch marks are going to be worth a fortune!" I laughed with them.

"Let me show you how to do it 'Liza." Jamie said, as he picked up my sketchbook. He started drawing a picture of me in my wheelchair. "Now you look beautiful!"

"That I do!" I laughed. "You are a great artist, Jamie. I couldn't have done it better myself!"

"Mom and Dad, could you do me a big favor? Could you contact Jobella and her husband, Steve? I would like to see if they could come see me. I want them to meet with my friends and me, for one of our Bible studies. Also could you find out what happened to Eric Evans, my physical therapist I had at the hospital? I've been worried about him ever since the accident with the elevator. I want him to know where I am."

"We'll try to see if we can find them. Maybe when Eric gets back to work at the hospital I'll be able to find him easier, but I don't know when that will be yet. I'll check with Steve's parents to see how to reach them. I don't know if they have a new number for them yet. In the meantime, why don't you try to send them an email, or look for them on Facebook?

"I didn't even think about that! Jobella maybe on Facebook, but I don't know if Eric has an account or not. I guess I can try to see if he's on there. I never thought about going on it and looking people up that way. I actually just signed up for an account and I don't know how to use it yet. Thank you for the suggestion. I'll try it, but still see what you can do about calling them. I want to talk with them. Speaking of friends, have you heard anything about Billie and Zoe?"

"Billie has her casts off now, but she still has a bad limp. They are doing therapy with her to try to correct that. Her left arm is doing okay, but she doesn't have much strength in it yet. It's a good thing that she's right handed! Zoe is out of her coma now and they moved her to a private room, but then she had to be moved to another hospital because of the earthquake damage. Her mother told me that physically she was doing all right. They've removed the chest tubes and the monitors, but they don't think she'll ever be normal again mentally because of the brain damage she suffered due to the lack of oxygen during her codes. Her mother said she is almost like a child in her thinking. She'll have to relearn basic stills again, as well. It's sad really, for her and her family."

"I'm so sorry to hear that about her. Would you let her, and her family know that I'll be praying for them? I'll be praying for Billie also. I'll check about seeing if Billie is on Facebook as well, after I figure out what I'm doing, that is."

Later that night I signed into Facebook and started looking for my friends. I don't know why I never thought to do it before. I guess I was too busy with school and other activities to make the time for it. Now it seems, I had all the time in the world. After I figured out how to set it up, and invite friends, I was ready to use it. Several people came to mind and I sent friend requests to everyone I knew. Jobella was first on my mental list, then Billie, Zoe, and several others I knew from school. I also added my parents even though I saw them every night. I typed in Eric's name as well and was happy that he too, had an account. I invited him to be my friend. I didn't know if I would ever hear from him again, but I had to at least give it a try.

Before going to bed, I decided to read my Bible. I found several verses that had to do with people with disabilities. The verses would be a good start to share with my new friends at our Bible study tomorrow.

In Second Corinthians 12:9 it says:
And he said unto me, My grace is sufficient for thee: for my strength is made perfect in weakness. Most gladly therefore will I rather glory in my infirmities, that the power of Christ may rest upon me.

In Romans 5:3-5:5:
And not only (so), but we glory in tribulations also: knowing that tribulation worketh patience; and patience, experience; and experience, hope: and hope maketh not ashamed; because the love of God is shed abroad in our hearts by the Holy Ghost which is given unto us.

In Hebrews 12:12-12:14:
Wherefore lift up the hands which hang down, and the feeble knees; and make straight paths for your feet, lest that which is lame be turned out of the

way; but let it rather be healed. Follow peace with all (men), and holiness, without which no man shall see the Lord:

As I fell asleep that night, I thought of those verses, each one reaffirming the fact that God truly loves his afflicted children. I submitted myself to prayer as I thought on these things.

"God, I know you are real. I thank you, even in my paralysis, that you saved me after I ran away from you and did everything I could to deny your existence. Forgive me Lord for ever doubting your love for me. I know it wasn't necessarily your will for me to get in that accident and become crippled and being in that elevator just as the earthquake hit so I was confronted with my own mortality, and then being moved into this place to meet Akeylia and Katelyn. I do know, as you said in your word in 'Romans 8:28: And we know that all things work together for good to them that love God, to them who are the called according to his purpose'. So maybe you did want me here in this place, just at this time. Help me Lord, to fully accept my condition, and show me how I can do your will. In Jesus name I pray, amen.

He answered me that night by speaking to my heart. 'Daughter, all things are done according to my purpose. I love you, and though this happened to you, it will be for the greater good to further my kingdom. You will regain some of the strength in your body, but your body is not you. It's just a vessel to house your soul. Your greatest strength will come from your heart. You will do many things in your life to bring honor to me. You will become a witness to others like you who need your testimony. You'll bring many more souls into my kingdom because of your infirmity. Akeylia will become a Christian because of your words, and your love for her. It is essential that you lead her to me soon. Now go rest in peace.

Chapter 16

It was the middle of October when Eric left the hospital. It was two weeks after the earthquake that caused so much damage at the hospital where he worked.

He finally recognized his family and was anxious to get home so he could recoup the rest of his memories. He felt he could only do that in familiar surroundings.

As soon as they drove up the driveway, Toby came running out to greet him. He knelt down to give him a big hug. "Hi boy, did you miss me?" Toby answered him by jumping into his arms and showering him with licks to his face, and a wildly wagging tail. "I guess that would be a yes," he laughed.

After he went inside, he looked around the house and started toward his old bedroom with his parents.

"So, are you starting to remember this place at all?" His dad asked.

"It's coming back. I remember my bedroom is at the top of the stairs, is that right?" He had moved out a few years back when he went away to college. He only used the room when he came home for visits. His parents tried to keep it the same way so when he came home from college he could still use it and be comfortable in it. They also used his room for guests once in a while.

"Yes, it is." Said his mother, with tears in her eyes. She was so happy that he was recognizing more things about his past.

He glanced around his room. His football jerseys and trophies from high school and college were still displayed in a case next to his bed and he had a picture of each of the football teams in frames sitting on his dresser along with a picture of his family and one of him with Toby. He even had a picture of Toby with his broken hind legs in casts. When he saw that picture he remembered working with him until he was totally healed and could run and play like before.

Seeing the football paraphernalia reminded him of his football days, both in high school and in college, and then came the not so pleasant thoughts of his partying days with his so-called friends from college. He was glad he was saved by God and was no longer in that crowd. He touched the coolness of the metal on the trophies and ran his finger over the engravings that proclaimed him being the most valuable player. Then he picked up the football and felt the rough surface of the pigskin against his skin. He held it like he was going throw it and remembered how good it felt to be the star quarterback. Sometimes he missed the roar of the crowds and playing football.

As he thought back to his high school days, he started remembering about how he let his family down and how he distanced himself from them...until he got his dog. By the time he left for college, he was getting along great with all of them and actually hated to leave them for school. He then remembered some of the things he learned in college and how his life had spiraled downhill until he became a Christian. School started going a lot better after that and he eventually was able to graduate early.

After a few days of recovering at home, he started getting a little restless. He was feeling better now and he wanted to go back to his rented house and make sure everything was okay there. He also wanted to go by the hospital and see if there was anything he could do to help get it back in working order. He thought that it would stir up the memories of what happened there and maybe even recall the girl that he was helping when he was injured.

His mother went with him as he drove. She wanted to make sure he still remembered how to get to his house. She was afraid he wouldn't remember where he lived and get lost trying to get there. After one wrong turn, it started to come back to him. He noticed some landmarks along the way, like his old high school and the church he went to. After driving a few more blocks, he would be there. Once he got his bearings, he remembered where his house was.

He glanced around after he entered his house. A magazine about physical therapy lying on his table triggered his memory about his job. He decided to take it back to his parent's house so he could look through it. Maybe the articles would remind him of some of the things about his job.

After leaving the apartment, he and his mother went to the hospital to see how they were coming with the repairs. They didn't know if they would be allowed inside because of the construction, but it wasn't as bad as they thought it would be. It had been two weeks since the earthquake and the crews had been working around the clock to get it back up and functioning again.

They proceeded first to the therapy department to see how everything was going. A few of the people he worked with were helping to get everything cleaned up and ready to use again. A goal had been set for the hospital to reopen by the end of the week.

A man wearing overalls came up to Eric and shook his hand and patted him on the back. "Hi, we're glad to have you back."

"Do I know you?" Eric asked. "You look familiar, but I don't remember anyone working here that has long hair and a beard."

"Eric don't you know me? I'm you're boss, Christopher Shepherd. I heard you are having memory problems since you were knocked out, but I figured you'd be okay by now."

"It's good to see you again, Chris." I said, although I still couldn't quite place him. "I'm afraid I'm still a little dull in the memory department, but it's coming back in bits and pieces. I thought that if I came and looked around it would help."

"Go ahead and look around all you want. If you need anything let me know. Reintroduce yourself to everyone, and if you want to check out the equipment, that will be fine as well."

Eric walked over to the computer with the crazy looking pedaling gizmo attached to it. "How does this work?" he asked Chris.

Chris turned it on and he saw a forest scene with a dirt path on the screen. "Now put your hands on the pedals and move them like you're riding a bike, only with your hands."

Eric started peddling and all of a sudden he had a flash of a memory. He remembered working with a beautiful girl that had a broken neck. She just had surgery a few days before he brought her down to start her on shoulder strengthening exercises. Thoughts kept flashing through his brain like electrical sparks. He suddenly remembered he was with this girl when the elevator stopped during the earthquake, and the ceiling fell on his head and knocked him out. Now, if he could only remember her name. She had to have been moved from the hospital because no one was allowed to stay.

"Chris, you don't happen to remember the name of the girl I was training do you? She was a quadriplegic."

"I'm not sure, there are so many people that go through here. You can check your log over on your desk. It should still be there. I haven't moved any of your things yet."

When he checked his logbook, one name kept coming up each day, Eliza Goodman. *That has to be her'* He thought. *Maybe, if I contact her parents, I can find out what happened to her'.*

He wrote her name down on a piece of paper, stuffed it in his pocket, and then looked around at some more of the equipment before he left the area. When he tried to find Chris, to thank him, he was nowhere in sight. He figured that maybe he went somewhere to eat lunch.

He said goodbye to some of the other staff, but when he asked about where Chris had gone, because he wanted to thank him, none of them seemed to know who he was talking about.

"There's no one here by that name." smiled one of the assistants. "I think I would have remembered someone like that."

He walked out the door of the gym and met up with his mother. "Did you see anyone come out of here with a beard and ponytail?" He asked.

"No, you're the only one I've seen."

"I found out the name of the girl I was looking for. I'd like to see if I could find her, to let her know I'm okay."

"I'll help you if you want me to, but that is probably something you would rather do yourself."

After they went back to his parent's house, he set to work trying to find out where in the world Eliza Goodman could have been taken to. There were several listings for Goodman in the phone directory, but he wasn't sure what her parent's names were and there definitely wasn't a listing for an Eliza Goodman. He wasn't even sure if she was from the local area. It seemed like a daunting task trying to find her. He thought about checking for her on Facebook but even if she had an account, would she be able to communicate with him? Was she even able to use a computer with her limited ability?

As he was thinking of her, he began to wonder why it was so important to get in touch with her. She was only one of his many patients, so why was she so different? Why was getting in touch with her so important? He shrugged it off. Maybe it was just because she was with him when he was hurt. Surely that was it. Maybe if he saw her again he could bring closure to this incident.

Chapter 17

The next morning after I prayed, then got an answer from God, and after reading the Bible text referring to handi-capped people the night before, I was anxious to start my Bible study with Akeylia and Katelyn.

The Bible study time would have to wait until after lunch because the mornings were given to my therapy. Sam came in to give me my bed bath and then I was put in my wheelchair to eat breakfast. After breakfast they came to get me for my therapy time. They worked with me for about an hour each day. They continued to do range of motion exercises with my legs and arms and then my shoulder exercises on the 'bike'. My shoulders were getting a little stronger now so they had me start on the gradual uphill course on the computer. It was a little harder to pedal, but it would increase my strength in my shoulders. As I was going through the exercise, the tingling feeling came back in my hands again, raising my hopes that maybe I could still eventually get some feelings back. After the pedaling, the therapist started doing my shoulder lifting exercises trying to get me to move my hand around. I was able to lift it a little higher today, maybe an inch to an inch and a half.

"You're doing good Eliza, when we get you up to two inches and see if you can move objects, we'll start looking for an electric wheelchair for you."

"When are we going to do the exercises to move objects?"

"We'll start on that tomorrow, Unfortunately our time is up for today. You can start practicing on your own, but without wearing a brace for leverage, at least in the beginning, you will probably not have much luck."

After lunch, Akeylia and Katelyn dropped by right on schedule for our Bible study.

"How are you all doing?" I greeted them, smiling.

"What are you so happy about, just because we're having Bible study? I feel like I'm back in school. I suppose you're going to give us homework too." Akeylia frowned.

"Don't pay any attention to Akeylia, Eliza. She's feeling down in the dumps today for some reason, personally for me, I'm excited to be here!" added Katelyn.

"Has anything different happened to you, Akeylia, what's the matter?" I asked.

"I didn't sleep well, and I think I'm coming down with something." She replied.

"Well, we don't have to meet that long and you can leave when ever you like."

"I should be able to stay for a while. I'm sorry. I'm just feeling a little down today. I hate that the three of us are like this. I care for you all but I feel so helpless and useless!" Akeylia started to tear up. I would hug her and try to make her feel better, if I could. Katelyn rolled over to her and gave her a hug for both of us.

"Did something happen to you to make you feel sadder today?" I asked.

"Nothing in particular, after some of our discussions I've started wondering about things. Like is there life after death and if there isn't, is this all there is to our lives? What makes you and Katelyn able to smile when you are no better off than I am? Am I missing something?"

"Akeylia, do you mind if I say a prayer for us before we start our study?"

"Go ahead, I know you're going to whether I want you to or not."

We bowed our heads and I prayed. "Dear Heavenly Father, be with us now, as we study your word. Thank you for my friends in this place and what you are going to reveal to us through our sharing, and in reading your word. Be with Akeylia. Help her feel better both physically and emotionally. We pray for her salvation and we pray that she can take something away from our Bible study that will help her feel a need in her life. Open our hearts to your leading now. In Jesus name I pray, amen."

We decided to use the verses I found the night before, to start our study in. I shared with them the passages of Second Corinthians 12:9, Romans 4:3-5, and Hebrews 12:12-14. All of them spoke to those with afflictions and tribulations and how those problems could be used to bring us to a closer walk to Christ. It said that God's strength would be made perfect in our weakness. I also shared that I heard a voice in my heart after I prayed. I felt God telling me that our bodies were only a vessel to hold our souls and our soul is what matters. We need to uplift each other and stand firm in what we believe. We need to share what God has done in our lives. In reading those verses from Paul's epistles, I remembered somewhere that Paul talked about the thorn in his side. The Bible doesn't say what the thorn was, but it evidently was a problem for Paul. It could have even been a handicap for him. Whatever it was, he turned it over to God.

We went on to share our stories of salvation with one another and I watched Akeylia as we gave our testimonies.

Katelyn spoke first: "I grew up in the church. My dad was a preacher and it was all I never knew. I didn't know what it was to live outside of the church and our Christian family. One summer…when I was a teenager, I went to Bible camp and our counselor took a group of us off to a sheltered area in the woods to talk with us in a small group setting. He told us that it wasn't enough for us to grow up in the church and have the knowledge of God, but we had to give it all to him; our heart, soul, mind, and yes, even our body. I guess I thought that because my parents were saved I would automatically be also, but then, I started thinking about all of the impure thoughts that had gone through my brain. I thought I was better than anyone else and I looked down on others, even on the kids I went to church with. Don't even get me started on the kids at school who didn't go to church at all. I started hanging out with the preppy girls in high school and college, you know, the ones who were always hanging all over the popular guys. I even had a few dates that I'm embarrassed to say, I did some not so godly things, before they ended. One night while I was still in high school, I even stayed at a boy's house when his parent's weren't there and then lied to my mother and told her that I was studying at a friend's house and fell asleep on her sofa. Well, when I got thinking of all those things, I felt ashamed. I knew then that my life didn't belong to Christ and I wanted to make sure that I was saved. That's when I got down on my knees, bore my soul to him, and I became saved. I never cried so hard in my life, but it was a good cry. I knew from that time on I belonged to Jesus, my home in heaven was a certainty, and my salvation was assured. Shortly after that, I was diagnosed with multiple sclerosis. I was sixteen years old at that time. I've been living with this disease for going on eight years now, but I have never had doubts about God's love for me, even with this affliction. I know he has a reason for me being here now, and I praise him for it."

After she was finished, I told them about my conversion. "My story is similar to Kate's. I grew up in church as well. My parent's were pretty active until I was my late teens. When my friends and I got tired of going and being hypocrites, my parents decided that they weren't going any more as well. That's when I really started getting in trouble. I partied too much, starting right out of high school. My parents were almost sent to jail because I allowed my friends to drink at our house. One of those friends even died in a car wreck that night. Another time, I spent the night with my boyfriend after telling them I was at my friend's house and had her lie to them, to back up my story. I was scared to death that I was pregnant, but thankfully, I wasn't. When I went to college, I almost lost my scholarship because I showed up with hangovers all the time to our field meets. All of this time I had a head knowledge of Christ and his forgiveness but I didn't have it in my heart. I never gave my life to him. I didn't want to feel convicted because of my lifestyle. I thought I was having too much fun. But sometimes God has to literally knock you in the head to get your attention." I smiled when I said that. "Then it happened, two of my best friends and I were riding in a car in heavy rain and we hydroplaned across the median and were hit by an eighteen-wheeler. I became extremely bitter toward God after the accident, especially when I found out that I would be crippled for the rest of my life. Well...after a couple of surgeries, the comforting words of friends who were Christians, and especially my physical therapist, who was a Christian as well, I became more encouraged that maybe my disability wasn't the end. Shortly after my second surgery, when I was getting into a routine of going to therapy everyday, my therapist came and got me early one day, and as we headed down the elevator the earthquake hit and all the lights went out. My therapist was knocked out by falling debris and I couldn't wake him up. We were stuck in the elevator for a couple of hours in complete darkness and I thought I was going to die. I prayed to God and I gave my life to him. On that elevator I realized that when everything is taken from us, the only thing we have left is God. God must have sent an angel that day to protect my therapist and me. There was no other way to explain how the staff heard the emergency alarm when I wasn't able to push it and all the electricity was off so it wasn't even functioning. If I had any doubts at all they vanished that day and I was saved in my spirit as well as my physical body."

"I don't really believe any of that stuff. I don't believe anything I can't see or feel. God's just not real to me. I go to church here in the nursing home and I can see the joy it brings to those that come to the services. The music is great and like I said before, it's something to do with the others. It's just a diversion to me in an otherwise boring place."

"That's why they call it faith, believing in something that's there, but you can't see it. It's kind of like the wind, you can't see it but you know it's there because you see the trees sway. You can't see God, but you can see the way he affects people's lives. Akeylia, what do you believe?" I asked.

"I think it is something parent's and church people talk about to make people behave. It's kind of like Santa Claus or the Easter bunny. If you don't believe and you misbehave, they won't bring you anything. I believe they are made up too and are as real as God. Sorry, I guess I just don't buy it."

"Akeylia, if you were to die tonight, where would you spend eternity?" Katelyn suddenly asked.

"I guess I'd be rotting in a coffin, same as everyone else, or my ashes would be in a jar somewhere."

"Do you believe in Christ?" I asked. I could tell we were making her a little uncomfortable, but I didn't want to give up on her.

"Of course, I believe in a man called Jesus. I know he lived two thousand years ago. He was a great teacher and taught a lot of things about how to live, and yes I know he was crucified and supposedly came back to life." She replied.

"Do you believe he lied when he talked about heaven and hell? Do you believe the stories where he healed the blind, the lame that couldn't walk, and those that were possessed by demons?" I asked.

"Yes I read those stories too. I did pay attention in church once in a while, but I don't see anything like that happening now except by those television evangelists that have those fake healings, and try to take your money."

"But God still heals people. There have been many times when someone is on the brink of death and because people prayed over them, they are healed. Miracles still happen. By all rights, I should've been dead from the accident I was in, but God saved me because he had a job for me to do. My friends that were with me should have died as well. One of them came to visit me while I was in the hospital. She claimed that she saw angels in the car with us, keeping us from the full impact of the wreck. Another friend actually had a near death experience. She claimed angels took her to heaven and she saw Jesus, angels, and even her family members that had died. So I can tell you that heaven is for real, and there is an afterlife. I know I can't save you, I can only pass on what I know and share God's love with you. I also know that until you feel God's love and intervention in your life, you won't believe anything we're trying to tell you. Trust me, I didn't believe either until I really had a heart to heart talk with him that day in the elevator. God did specifically tell me to talk with you when I prayed last night. He loves you, Akeylia, I can tell you that. I'm going to continue to pray for you and I know that Katelyn will as well."

"I'll keep everything you told me in my heart. I'll read my Bible to find out what I'm missing, and yes, I'll even give praying a chance. But right now, I guess I'd better go back to my room. I'm getting really sleepy and I'm in a lot of pain through my back today. Thank you for your friendship, you both mean so much to me. I'm sorry I'm so negative about religion. I just never really thought about things the way you two have."

After Akeylia left, my heart felt heavily burdened for her. I shared my feelings with Katelyn, and we decided to finish our time of sharing with prayer for our friend. We both felt that God was doing something in both of our lives, leading us into some type of Christian service, and of course, our most immediate concern was to lead Akeylia to Christ before it was too late.

Chapter 18

A few days later my parents and Jamie dropped by to see me. I had been doing some drawings in my sketchbook earlier in the day. I was getting a little better with my drawings as I practiced more. I had been drawing some flowers and tried to write a short poem to go with it. It was still very rough looking, but it looked more like an older child drew it instead of a toddler.

"You're really getting pretty good at that whole mouth drawing thing you do." Dad said. "Pretty soon you'll be better than me!"

"I don't think so, Dad. Drawing straight lines will never be something I can handle!" I laughed.

"Well I guess I won't be able to sign you on to be an architect then." He smiled. "I guess you could always fill in the landscape though. You could draw the flower gardens. I'm terrible with that."

"You may have a point there, I'll think about it!" Actually, that didn't sound like a bad idea.

"I heard that you are getting an electric wheelchair soon, that's exciting!" Mom said.

"It's supposed to be here tomorrow or the next day. When it comes in, I'll start practicing with it. I've been working on moving my hand around using the muscles in my upper arms. I'm getting pretty good at that." I showed them how I could move my television remote, and even press the buttons on it. I raised my hand, and slide the remote a good two inches. "The therapist told me that I would be able to maneuver the controls on the wheelchair by moving my hand like that. It's going to take a lot of practice, though."

"Well, we have a surprise for you as well. We've finally started on the renovations for the house. They've finished with the hospital now, so I was able to finally get a contractor." Dad smiled.

"How long do you think it will be until they're finished?"

"The contractor said that it would be approximately a month. Maybe by the time you get use to your new chair, we will be ready to get you home. We've also been looking into getting a new van with a lift so we can take you places. Your mother is also going to look into getting a second shift position at the hospital so she can be there in the daytime for you and I can be with you in the evenings. I know you're ready to get out of this place." He said.

"I'm getting use to it. They're doing a good job taking care of me and besides I've made a couple of new friends here, I'll miss them when I leave."

"That's right, I heard that you all started a Bible study, how's it going?" Mom asked.

"It's great, Katelyn and I have been trying to talk with Akeylia, and we've praying for her because she isn't saved. I'm concerned for her because God laid it on my heart that she needed to accept Christ soon. The last couple of days she hasn't come. Katelyn said that she is sick. Please pray for her before it's too late."

"Speaking of prayer, we decided to go back to church, Eliza. After what happened to you we felt a need to get back into fellowship with our church friends and especially with God. We also wanted to make sure that Jamie would have a Christian base to live his life on. It was hard at first because we have been out of the 'habit' of going for a few years, but they accepted us back with open arms. They've been praying for us and especially for you."

I was so thankful that they rededicated their lives. It brought tears to my eyes. After all, it was my stubbornness and lack of faith that made them stop going to start with. Mom wiped my eyes with a tissue and gave me a hug.

"I'm so happy you did that, getting back in church, I mean." I said. "Have you heard anymore from my friends? I really miss them. I wish they would come and visit me."

"Well I've not seen Eric back at the hospital yet. I checked with the therapy department. They said he stopped by one day to check out how the renovations were going so I know he's doing better physically. I'm sure that Jobella and Steve are busy now that they are both in school, and I'm not sure about Zoe and Billie. Billie of course is back home but Zoe went to another hospital and I haven't been in touch with her parents so I'm not sure what's happening with her. Why don't you try to reach them through your computer?" Mom asked.

"I almost forgot about that. I'll do it later after you leave."

"I'm looking into getting you a 'hands-free' phone as well. When I looked up things on the Internet for disabled people, I was amazed at what all was out there. You can actually live a fairly normal life with everything they have nowadays." Dad said.

"That will be great! Thanks dad for checking into all of those things. I guess I could check things out as well and let you know if there is something else I would be especially interested in."

After we said our goodbyes, I settled down with my I-pad again and went to look at my Facebook page. I had several people who wanted to be my friends. I started clicking 'confirm' on several of them. My mom and dad were on there of course, as well. Who would have thought that they would be so hip on all this new stuff? No wonder they were so anxious for me to try it out. Following them there was Jobella and Billie and several of my friends from college and high school and then I saw him, Eric Evans.

I quickly typed his name in the search box and confirmed him as a friend. I was surprised when he contacted me a few minutes later. Why didn't I think of this sooner!

I went into a private chat room with him. He told me what happened and about being moved to another hospital and how he lost his memory from the injury to his head. He said that he finally remembered a girl he was treating but couldn't remember her name up until a few days ago. He told me he went by the rehab department where he worked and saw my name on his logbook but he still didn't know how to get in touch with me, so he was excited that I contacted him.

I told him that I was at Sunnyside Woods nursing home and I was continuing in therapy and I was finally going to get my electric wheel chair soon. After I could get around and my parent's finished remodeling the house, I would be able to go home. I told him also about how I became a Christian and was now doing a Bible study with two other girls.

Then he told me that he missed me and wanted to come to visit me, if I was up to it, of course.

Wow, did I ever want to see him again! Was he kidding? We made plans for the very next day. He said he'd come around at 3:00, if I wasn't too busy at that time. He said he hadn't gone back to work yet, but he was helping the staff at the hospital get things back in order and he also wanted to refresh his memory of what to do with some of the equipment, but he could leave whenever he wanted since he was volunteering to do the work.

When he signed off he said he loved me. If my legs were functioning, I would have jumped up and started dancing around the room…he said he loved me.

I didn't sleep very well that night. I was so excited that Eric and I had finally connected. I was a little worried about his expectations when he finally did see me. I looked a little bit different then the last time he saw me. The last time we were together I had a baldhead from where they had to shave me before putting me in traction and I wore a woolen cap to cover up my stubble and scars. I also sported a neck brace and had residual bruising from my surgeries and accident. If he could love me looking like, than I hoped I would look a little better to him now. My hair had grown out about an inch and my surgical scars were gone and I no longer had to wear a neck brace.

The next morning I awoke and despite not sleeping well, I was wide-awake and excited about the day ahead. I couldn't wait until Eric came, but before he did, I still had to go to therapy, get a bath, and later have my Bible study with my friends.

I asked Sam if I could get a whirlpool bath that day so I would feel good and fresh, and put me in a nice outfit, and toward time for him to come, if she would put a little <u>makeup</u> on me.

She just laughed, "So you have a hot date, huh?"

"That would be a yes. My physical therapist from the hospital is coming to see me! You remember, the one we talked about after I was first admitted."

"I remember, I'm glad he's finally well, and he remembered you."

"Me too, Sam, he is such a nice guy and good looking as well! I can't believe that he is interested in me with all my problems!"

"As a therapist, I'm sure he sees all kinds of people with all kinds of problems and you said he's a Christian, right? He's looking past the exterior and is looking at you, Eliza, at you, not your body. He's looking here… and here." She said pointing to my head and my heart.

"Maybe he just cares as a friend, right? Surely he's not into me for the long term. Guy's don't want to have someone that they have to wait on hand and foot, literally." I frowned.

"You let him make that decision. Just let it happen, Eliza. God knows your heart and his. If it's to be, it'll be."

"Thanks, Sam. I really appreciate your kindness and your words of encouragement. Now let's make me beautiful!" I laughed.

After lunch Katelyn came to my room for Bible study. Akeylia wasn't with her again. It had been a week since she came to meet with us.

"Where's Akeylia?" I asked. "Did we upset her so much she didn't want to come anymore?"

"So you haven't heard, then. They took Akeylia out in an ambulance yesterday afternoon. Her oxygen level got dangerously low. They think she has pneumonia. She was almost blue when they took her. I told the nurse to let me know if something happens to her. Oh Eliza, we really need to pray for her. I don't know if she ever accepted Christ or not. She never told me."

"So, let's spend this time lifting her up to God and praying that she will get better, okay?"

"Dear Heavenly Father," Katelyn began. "Be with our sister and friend, Akeylia. She is hurting now. Please be with the doctors and nurses and help them to make the right decisions on how to help her best. Father, most of all we pray that if she hadn't made a profession of faith, that through this ordeal she will see her need for you. She has gone through so much in her life and is skeptical about believing and trusting in you. Please Lord if it be your will, she will survive this ordeal she's going through now and give her the opportunity to come and know you, even now. In Jesus name I pray, amen."

Then I continued to pray. "Lord, my heart hurts for Akeylia, please let her get better. We would really like her to get to know you more and accept that you are real. Lord, I know that you are able to heal her body and her spirit. Father, what a great testimony it would be to her if she would be healed, when everything is against it, to be so. Lord, only you can bring her back from the brink of death as you have done before, even with my friends and me. She needs to see that you are real, and she can trust in you. Lord please grant her the strength to fight off this illness she has now. Don't give up on her, God. She needs you! Amen."

Now all we could do was wait on God's amazing power to do his work in Akeylia's life. Before Katelyn left, we turned everything over to the Lord because when it comes down to it, the only thing we could do now is to pray and comfort each other.

I was so thankful to have Katelyn as a friend. We really helped buoy each other up in times like these. I hoped the nurse knew now close we had gotten to our friend and would let us know if there were any changes.

After our prayer time and short visit, it was almost time for Eric to come by. I was so nervous, if I could move, my knees would be rattling, and I would be shaking in my boots. I hadn't seen him in over a month and I hoped that he would have a few good memories of me, even if I was a mess and outwardly opposed to being a Christian. I knew he would be excited when he found out that I became one, as well. At least we would have that in common.

I kept watching the clock. At half past two, it seemed to have stopped. I decided to read a few verses in the Bible to help me pass the time. I read anything I could find about angels. I was surprised to learn that they were mentioned over two hundred seventy times in the Bible. That would be a great undertaking to learn about them and everything they did to further the kingdom. Then I prayed a quick prayer to God to have His angels watch over Akeylia.

Chapter 19

T he next thing I knew there was a knock on the door. "Come in." I called through the closed door.

"Are you decent?" Eric laughed.

"About as much as I can be. Get in here, you've made me wait long enough!" I laughed back.

He walked through the door holding a gorgeous bouquet of salmon color roses.

"Those are beautiful, but seeing you would have been enough of a gift." I smiled.

"Hey sunshine, I'm so glad to be finally here. I've really missed you. At least since I got my memory back and knew you were my favorite girl. Who knows how long it would have been if you hadn't looked me up on Facebook." He came over, gave me a big hug, and kissed me. "I like your hair like that. It looks like it would be easy to care for. It's really cute."

"I miss my long dark hair though, but unless I get a nurse to take care of me twenty-four-seven, it would be too hard to take care of."

"I talked with your folks. They told me that you became a Christian, that's great! You don't know how good that makes me feel. I've been praying for that ever since I met you. I knew you had great potential, and now God can use you, and develop that potential even further."

Then he noticed the painting on the wall. "I love the painting! I've never seen one like that before."

"My Mom got it for me. It's beautiful isn't it?"

"We need something like that in our gym at the hospital, but you know they wouldn't let us have anything like that hanging in a public place. They would be too worried about offending someone that wasn't a Christian." He replied.

"That's true. Even though the majority of Americans are Christians or believe that Christ was a real person, the few that don't believe seem to make up all the rules for the rest of us. It's so unfair! I think Christians ought to rise up and fight for our rights."

"I don't think that will ever happen. Satan has too much of a hold in the world today. Being a Christian just isn't enough anymore." Eric frowned.

"Then I say let's start making a difference one person at a time."

"I was hoping you'd say that because I was thinking about something. I was planning on running it by you and see if you'd be interested in working with me on it."

"Sure, as long it's something I can do in my condition."

"It's perfect for you in your condition. I've been thinking about starting an organization for disabled people. Maybe you can help me think about how to proceed with it, and you'd be vital in helping me run it."

"Okay, I'm game, but is that the only reason you are interested in me, because you want me to work with you, and be your poster girl?"

"Are you kidding me? Don't get me wrong, I didn't mean to make it sound like that. I want you to be with me because I'm in love with you, and I want you by my side to help other people. I fell for you the first time I saw you, and now that you're a Christian it makes it even better. Since I got my memory back, I've missed you like crazy."

"Me too. I'm glad to have you back in my life. I think I'm in love with as well, but I didn't think you'd love me in this condition!"

"You're condition has nothing to do with your heart or your brains. You have a lot of love to give. I'm just glad that some of that love is directed at me. I've had other girlfriends before, but no one has ever made me feel like you do."

"Aw, you're just saying that because you want me to work for you!" I laughed.

"No way! As a matter of fact, I'm going to check with your parents to see if I can take you for an outing tomorrow. I'd like to take you to meet my parents, and go to the park to have a picnic. We can talk a little more about what I have planned then, okay?"

"Sound's like fun, if it's alright with everyone."

"I'll be by around 11:00 tomorrow morning. That will give you time to have your therapy before we go. We'll drop by a fast food place and take it to the park for lunch. After we eat, we'll go for a walk in the woods and then afterwards I'll take you by my mom and dad's house. Sound like a plan?"

"Sounds good, but how will you transport me."

"You forget I'm a physical therapist. I deal with people in wheelchairs all the time. I'll take you out of the wheelchair and put you in the car and put your chair in the trunk. It won't be a deal for me."

"You'll have to feed me as well."

"No problem there either," he laughed. "Anymore excuses?"

I started laughing then. "Can't think of anything else, as long as you're sure."

"Alright, I'll be back tomorrow then. I'll get everything worked out with your folks and mine, and get the needed paperwork done at the front desk to take you out."

That night after supper, Mom and Dad came to see me. I told them all about Eric, and what he had planned for us to do tomorrow, and our future business of helping the disabled.

"He came by to see us," Dad said, "and told us about it as well. He is really a fine young man. I believe you two would do very well together in a business like that."

Mom added, "We're so happy for you. I really think he likes you a lot."

Jamie, not be outdone, said. "Are you two gonna' get married, 'Liza?"

"It hasn't got that far, Jamie." I laughed. "We're just going to the park to talk about our new business."

"Yeah, right!" he giggled.

Dad mussed up Jamie's hair and shushed him. "They're just friends."

After my nurse and nursing aide settled me into bed, I read for a while before turning my tablet off, and fell into a deep sleep. I was happier than I'd been since this whole ordeal started. I was beginning to finally feel like my life was going somewhere and there was a hope for the future.

The next day started out full of promise. I went to the therapy gym and saw that they finally got my wheelchair in. After two of the therapy aides lifted me into the chair, my therapist showed me the controls and how everything worked. It had a tall back on it so I could rest my head against it. On the armrests there were controls that I could move with my hands. At my right hand there was a type of joystick that would serve as a 'steering mechanism'. She showed me how I would lift my shoulder to raise my hand and then move it to the right or left. On my left hand was the accelerator and brake. Without turning the chair on, she let me play with the controls, just to see if I could move them. She had to put the special braces on my arms so that it would hold my fingers and lower arms in the right position to work the controls. It was kind of like having riding gloves on. We didn't have time to actually take it out for a test drive that day, but I was content to know that it was finally in and it belonged to me. It was kind of like getting a new car and getting use to it.

After playing with the electric wheelchair for a bit, she steered me over to the computer image, peddling machine. She turned up the intensity on it to make it feel like I was going up a steep hill. It was pretty hard to peddle my arms, but after a while I got use to it. My shoulders were getting a lot stronger now. I felt like I was getting a real workout.

We finished about 10:30, just in time for me to go get ready for Eric. Sam came and got me from therapy. I told her I needed to get ready for my 'date'.

"You going out with that guy that was here yesterday?" She asked while she was combing my hair and putting makeup on me.

"Yes, that was Eric. My therapist from the hospital."

"I can see why you were upset when you first got here and couldn't get in touch with him. That man is fine. You'd better hang on to him, and not let him get away!" She laughed.

"I honestly don't know what he sees in me. I don't even know if he considers me as his girlfriend. He wants to start some kind of organization for disabled people and wants me to be part of it."

"Honey, he could talk with you about his plans here. No, if he's taking you home to see his mama and daddy, he's seriously interested in you!" She rolled her eyes at me and I just had to smile.

Just as she was finishing up, Eric walked through the door. "Hi gorgeous, you ready to go?"

Sam stood at the door and smiled at me. She gave me a two-thumbs up sign and walked out.

It felt so good to get out of the nursing home for the afternoon. I almost forgot how beautiful the outside world was. After signing me out, Eric took me to his car. He had an SUV so it wasn't too bad getting in and out of it. After opening the door he slid me out of the wheelchair and over to the car seat and buckled me in. It wasn't as hard as I thought it would be. He really knew his business. He put the wheelchair in the trunk and we were on our way.

We stopped by a fast food place and got sandwiches, fries, and floats. We took it to the park to eat. He put the drink where I could reach it with a straw and he fed me the rest of the meal. It seemed heavenly after eating the food at the nursing home. Not that the food was bad there, it just doesn't taste the same as good old fast food.

After we ate. Eric pushed my wheel chair down one of the walking paths. It had a flat hard surface on one of the paths so people in wheelchairs could maneuver it with no problem. It felt good to be here again. I use to run here, so it brought back a lot of memories of the 'good ole days'.

"How's it feel to be outside again?" He asked.

"I'm loving it. Thank you for thinking of doing this. I use to run here when I was practicing for my cross-country races. It also reminds me of the first time you put me on that cycling computer program and you put your arms around me to steady my shoulders. This is way better though, I love the smell of the fresh air and listening to all the birds. I really do love being outside in God's beautiful world. Watching it on a TV screen or computer just isn't the same is it?"

"No it's not. I enjoy being outside too. One of my favorite things is to go camping and sitting around a campfire at night and cooking over the fire and eating s'mores."

"Sounds like fun, we'll have to do that someday."

"Actually that is something I'd like to do when we have our program going. I'm going to start taking a few religion classes at the local Bible college so that I can get some type of ministerial degree. I feel like God is leading me into doing a ministry with disabled and underprivileged people. Maybe we could have a sort of camp or ranch or something like that. I just have so many ideas, and I can't wait to get started!" Eric smiled at. "I want you to be part of it. Would you be willing to join me in that and support it, Eliza?" He asked.

"I would love that. I think it's a wonderful idea! I'm still not sure exactly what it is that I can do. I'm not much of a hands-on person now, if you catch my drift." I laughed.

"Don't worry. I'll still be your trainer. After you leave the nursing home, I will still continue to work with you. I'll make sure you become everything God wants you to be."

"You sound like you're making a long time commitment to me with all these plans."

"That's up to you, it can be as long as you are willing to be with me," he smiled.

After a few more minutes of sitting and enjoying each other's company, he took me back to the car and we left to go to his parent's house.

His parents lived in a beautiful home in the upper class neighborhood of Clairmonte. His father was a doctor and must have been a good one, because their house was huge.

"Do you think your parent's will like me? I'm sure I'm a lot different than your other girlfriends."

"What's not to love? Besides, I've never liked anyone else enough to take them home with me to meet them. They know all about your condition, so no worries there, okay?"

When we pulled up in the driveway, Eric put me in my wheelchair and took me up to the front door. Luckily there were no steps going into the house so it was easy passing through the threshold.

His Mom greeted me. "Hi, you must be Eliza, Eric told us all about you. It's so good to finally meet you. Welcome to our home."

His dad greeted us as well and showed us into the most beautiful den I had ever seen. It was all windows on one of the walls and a stone fireplace covered another entire wall. On the mantle above the fireplace were many family pictures. Eric handed them down where I could see them better and he told me about his younger brother and sister that were in the photographs. They were both teenagers and they must have been in school at the time we were visiting.

Toby came running in to greet us. Eric introduced me to his dog. It was very obvious that he was happy to see his master. He came up to sniff me and then go back to Eric like he couldn't decide if he liked me or not. Finally he came over to me and sat beside me and laid his head in my lap. How I wish I could've petted him. He was a real sweetheart. Eric told me the story of how he helped him after his accident and how he wanted to be a therapist after that. Eric had him stand so I could reach his sweet face with mine.

"Do you have any pets, dear?" asked his mother.

"I have a cat named Snickers. Mom and Dad are caring for him while I'm in the nursing home. I just got him about a month before my accident. He's not fully grown yet. I miss him like crazy, so Mom and Dad brought me a stuffed toy cat to lie on my bed to remind me of him. I can't wait until I can get back home.

I'll be so glad to see him again. I just hope he remembers me." I said with a tear in my eye.

"That shouldn't be too much longer, now. When I talked with your dad, he said the renovations were coming along well. He thought it might only be a couple more weeks." Eric replied.

"I really don't mind it too much at the nursing home now. I guess I'm getting use to it. I know I need more therapy, and I need to learn how to use my electric wheel chair, but I still I think I'll be able to recover better at home."

"When you do get home, maybe I can come by after work to help you with your exercises so you don't get too stiff and contracted."

"I don't want you to have to do that. You have a life to live without me being a burden to you. My mom will be there, and she can be taught to do that."

"Maybe that is something I want to do. Besides it will give me a chance to see you, and get to know you better. It's not a burden to help somebody you care for."

"You're sweet to want to help me."

After we talked a little longer, we said our goodbyes. I really enjoyed visiting with his family. They were very kind and they didn't seem to mind that I was crippled. Whether they wanted me as a girlfriend for their son, I couldn't get a feel for that, but I was thankful for the visit and just spending time with them made me feel special.

It was suppertime when we got back to Sunnyside Woods. Eric signed me in and took me back to my room. The mood seemed more somber than usual when I passed through the corridors. The nurses and aides seemed sad and as I rode by they looked at me and got quiet.

Chapter 20

"I wonder what's going on. Why is everyone so quiet?" I asked Eric.

"I'll see if I can find out anything," he said.

He walked around the facility to see if anyone knew anything. He came up on Katelyn riding around the corner, to see if I had gotten back in yet, because she had some news for me.

When he returned to my room he had Katelyn with him. I could tell that she had been crying. She had a letter in her hand.

"Oh Eliza," she sobbed. "Akeylia died in her sleep last night! Her mother brought in this letter that she wrote a few days ago. I'm so sad that we didn't get to say goodbye to her, but in reading this, I know she was thinking about us, even while she was sick."

She handed Eric the letter and I read it silently while he was holding it to where I could see it. There were a few tear stained splotches on it, probably from where her mother and Katelyn had read it. He read it along with me.

Dear Katelyn and Eliza,

If you are reading this letter, I've gone to be with the Lord. I'm sorry I missed the last few Bible studies with you guys, but I was really feeling sick, as you know. I did go ahead on with reading the Bible though, while I was in my room. I did a lot of studying and I found the scriptures in the New Testament that talked about being saved, especially the Roman Road to Salvation. I realized that I was a sinner, and that I needed the Lord. In my bed I prayed and ask Christ to be my savior and I asked for the forgiveness of my sins.

I wanted to thank you both for your witness to me. If it hadn't been for you two, I wouldn't be in heaven right now. Yes, I had a near death experience when I coded right after I arrived at the hospital. They brought me back from death and I recovered enough to write to you and have a chance to let you know what happened.

When I coded, my soul did leave my body and I was immediately taken to heaven. In heaven, I did see some angels and I saw Jesus. He was beautiful! Like nobody I've ever seen before. He had the kindest face. He reached out and touched me and my body was made whole again. There was no pain and

I could stand and walk and I even danced. Imagine that!

He told me I needed to go back and let you know what I saw so I could bring comfort to you, so you wouldn't be sad for me.

Well that's why I'm writing this letter, to let you know that you were right and I was wrong. Heaven is real and like I said, if you're reading this letter the angels came back for me. Don't cry for me because everything's all right now. I'll see you soon on this side. We can continue to be friends in this wonderful place. We'll all dance and sing together, and it will be fabulous. Just think, we will no longer be in pain and our bodies will be made whole again.

I love you all. I will miss you until you're here with me again.

Yours in Christ,
Akeylia Simmons.

Now I knew why there were tearstains on the letter. If the letter had been under my face instead of in front of it, my tears would have been added to it, the way they were pouring down my face right now. I was sad that she died, but I was grateful that she was able to accept Christ while she still could. It was a bittersweet moment. Katelyn and Eric both came to me to comfort me.

As the three of us sat and talked about some of the things that Akeylia had gone through in her life, I don't know who had the idea first, but we were all in agreement. When we started out talking about our new venture, we decided to name it after her. It would be called 'The Akeylia Simmons Foundation'.

After Eric kissed me goodbye and left, Katelyn and I continued to talk until the aides got us for supper. They decided to let me eat with Katelyn again because they knew that she would be lonely for Akeylia. It took a little extra time for the aide to set me up for supper and to feed me, but she said she didn't mind because she wanted us to be able to stay together. After I was finished, I sat and sipped on my tea while Katelyn was finishing up. The aide would come and get me after we were through visiting.

"Your boyfriend is really nice, Eliza. He has a really good idea about setting up a foundation in our friend's name. Do you know what he has planned yet?"

"I'm not sure. I just know he wants me to be a part of it and I believe he wants you to help as well. He took me to meet his parents today. They seemed to like me okay. His father is a doctor, a neurologist, I think. They must have a lot of money because their house is like a mansion!"

"That's not Dr. Ezekiel Evans is it?" she asked.

"Yes, I think that's what his name was, " I replied.

"Girl, he does have money! He's a world famous neurologist. I've actually gone to see him a few times! He's the one that finally diagnosed me with multiple sclerosis."

"So that's why they have such a nice house. I had no idea that's who he was. No wonder they weren't shocked at my paralysis. He probably works with a lot of people similar to me. They were both really nice. Of course, I haven't met his brother and sister yet, they must have still been in school."

"Maybe they can help us get the foundation going." Katelyn said. "I'm sure they would want to help out when they find out more about it."

After supper I went back to my room and waited for my parent's visit. I was anxious to let them know everything that happened today; about Eric's visit, the ride in the park, the visit with his parent's, and about the death of my friend. It truly was a day of hope and of sadness as well.

When I told them about the plans that Eric had, they became excited. It was going to be a great opportunity to help others like the Katelyn's and Akeylia's and even the permanently crippled of the world, like me.

"Let me know when he get's ready to start it, there may be something we can do to help." My dad said.

"Okay, I'll do that. I'm sure we'll need all the help we can get. Especially since there's not much I can do except give him moral support."

They were sad to learn about my friend, but they were happy that I was instrumental, along with Katelyn, in leading her to Christ. They thought it was a really neat idea to name our foundation for her.

After they left I settled down with my drawings. I tried to draw a picture of Akeylia, but it didn't turn out very good. I wanted to draw so much, but it just wasn't coming yet. It would continue to take a lot of practice.

I finally gave up on it, and had the staff put me to bed. It had been a very eventful day. I didn't realize just how tired I was until I finally got into the bed. I was going to read my Bible for a while, but I fell asleep by the time I read the first chapter.

Over the next two weeks every day was pretty much like the day before. I'd eat my breakfast, get my bath and then go to therapy. Every day I practiced with my electric wheelchair. When I first took it out for a 'spin' it was very awkward, I knocked over several cones and ran into the wall a few times. I was glad there wasn't anyone within a ten-foot radius of me or I would have knocked them over too. I started getting gradually better each day until I had good control over it. They finally gave me my 'license' to drive. I don't think it was an official North Carolina document, but it made me feel good that I was able to finally accomplish something concrete for myself, along with the fact that it was something I had to accomplish before they would allow me to go home.

Eric came by to see me every day now just like he said he would. He came directly from work so when he came he still had his scrubs on. He and I would go for a 'walk' through the court-yard. It was fall now and the trees were turning all shades of red, orange, and yellow. They decorated the gardens with fall flowers like mums and pumpkins. I love the fall, with its gorgeous colors and the cooler air felt great. I would have loved to walk through the leaves and feel them against my feet as they scattered with each step. I would just have to imagine the feeling as Eric did just that. To tease me, he picked up a handful of leaves and threw them at me and laughed. They actually felt good on my neck and shoulders.

It had been four months since my accident and I'd gone through a lot of changes. I was getting a little more mobile now that I had my electric wheelchair and I actually got around pretty good with it. When I went on outings with the staff at the nursing home or with Eric we usually took the regular wheelchair because it was just easier to fold it up and put it in the trunk. But in the facility, I rode around everywhere in the electronic chair. In therapy, they still worked on my range of motion exercises and the rehab aides still assisted me with my arm braces.

It had been about a month since my friend, Akeylia passed into heaven. Katelyn and I missed her a lot, but we knew she was better off where she is and that comforted us.

I was supposed to go home the next week and I worried about Katelyn. I was going to miss our daily Bible study. Eric said that he would come and get me and we could visit her at least once or twice a week, mostly on the weekends. I suggested to her that maybe she could get a pass and come to my house and visit as well. She thought that was a wonderful idea. Eric also thought that it would give the three of us a chance to discuss the business, 'a sort of board meeting' he said.

I was home by Thanksgiving. My mom was finally able to change to an evening shift position so she would be there to help me with getting up in the morning, and get my breakfast and lunch and dad would be there in the evening to help with supper and putting me to bed. I hated to continue to depend on them so much, but we had the routine down to a fine science now. Even getting in and out of the bed wasn't too bad. They would just put my wheelchair up next to the bed, scoot me to the edge of the bed, and slide me into it. From there I could get around the ground floor of our house. Dad had even rigged up the front door with kind of a garage door type opener, so all I had to do was press a button on a special remote he made for my chair, to open and close it. That way, if I wanted to go outside and they weren't there to help, I could go out on my own. Dad did make that ramp from the front door to the driveway, and he removed the thresholds going from one room to the next, and widened the doorways so that my wheelchair could get through them. He went through a lot of work to remodel our house for me, and I would always be grateful for that.

My room that he added on to the house was wonderful. It was on ground floor of course, and had large windows so that I could see what was going on outside. They bought me a hospital type bed that could be raised and lowered. My special desk and easel was set up in one corner so when I wanted to use it I could. There was another desk he had built for me to accommodate my wheelchair. He also got me a laptop computer with a touch screen and voice activation software. He got another wand with a rubber tip to use with my computer. My other one that I used with my I-pad was getting worn out with so much use.

My cat, Snickers, would come into bed with me and sleep with me at night. It was almost as if he knew that I couldn't feel him below my shoulders, because he would come up around my neck and face and rub up against my cheek and purr. Just like my stuff cat in the nursing home, only better. When I was sitting in my wheelchair, he would crawl into my lap and fall asleep.

We made a special wall space to hang my picture that Mom got me and she purchased other wall décor to go along with it. She bought me a plaque with the words *"I can do all things through Christ who strenghteneth me. Philippians 4:13"*. She also bought wall sconces and molded wall hangings that featured flying angels and flowers. They put houseplants around the room. The whole effect was beautiful. I loved my Mom and Dad so much for doing this room for me.

Thanksgiving was more special that year, because I could truly thank God for what he had done for me. I was glad when I smelled the great dinner Mom and Dad had cooked, and that I was home to enjoy it. It did make me feel sad because I wasn't able to help in the preparations. No one expected me to do anything but I could keep them company while they were cooking. I spent part of my time that morning writing a Thanksgiving Day prayer that I would share with them at dinnertime.

We had decided to invite Katelyn and her mom to eat with us. It was just the two of them. Her dad divorced her mom when Katelyn got sick. He couldn't handle the pressure of having a daughter with MS, so he just left. She didn't have any other relatives that lived close by. I was thankful that my mom and dad didn't have those issues over me. I believed that my condition actually brought them closer together. They were working as a team to help make my life easier and worth living.

I was so excited to see my friend. We went to my room while her mom went to the kitchen to help my mother. Katelyn loved my room.

"If I had a room like this I would never want to leave it!" she smiled. "You're so lucky to have your mom and dad being so supportive of you. My mom has to work two jobs just to keep me in the nursing home. She doesn't have a lot left over by the time she pays my monthly bill."

"I'm so sad to hear that. You've never mentioned that your dad left your family. That was so low of him! How did he think that your mom would be able to cope without him?"

"He was kind of a freeloader himself. He had a part-time job but they really depended on Mom's job. Even when he was there, he didn't do anything to take care of me. That's why Mom had to resort to putting me in a nursing home."

"Maybe when Eric get's our foundation up and running, he can help you out by giving you a job there. That may be a way you can help your mom out, and alleviate a little pressure off her."

"Has Eric said any more about it?" Katelyn asked.

"He's been kind of hush-hush about the whole thing. He's been talking to my dad for some reason, but he's not said anything else to me about it. Maybe there's obstacles concerning it and he doesn't want to discourage me."

"Or, maybe he's talking to your dad about the plans he has with you." She laughed.

"Don't be silly, he couldn't ever love me like that. I mean, just look at him, he's so handsome. He could have any girl he wants. Why would he love an invalid! I'm sure I'm just someone he wants to help when he starts his new business."

"Don't sell yourself too short, you're a beautiful person both inside and out. There's more to you than you realize!

After dinner our guests left and I was grateful for my friend. I prayed for her and her family's situation. I prayed that her father would see the light, and come back home to them.

Chapter 21

It was Christmas Eve now, and Eric was going to come and get me, to take me to the candlelight service at his church. He went to a different church from the one that I attended. He told me how beautiful the ceremony was and how he looked forward to going to it every year. He wanted me to share in it with him.

I'd been going to church more regularly at our home church since I've been home. We had our Christmas special music and play the weekend before Christmas, so we didn't have anything that evening. Last Sunday, I saw Jobella and Steve, her husband, as well as his parents, and a couple I never met before. Her little brother and sister were sitting with them. I also saw my friend Billie with her boyfriend. After church we had a time of fellowship together.

Jobella came over to me and hugged me. The twins were on her heels. "Eliza, you look great! What's been going on with you?" She asked.

"Well, after the earthquake, I spent a couple of months at Sunnyside Woods nursing center to finish my therapy, until Dad and Mom completed renovations on our house, to accommodate me and a wheelchair. I've been home about a month now. Eric, my physical therapist from the hospital has been real supportive of me, and has come to see me almost every day. He and I, and one of my friends from the nursing home, are planning on starting a Christian foundation for disabled people. We're going to start making plans for it after the first of the year. Eric's been looking into some things, but he hasn't shared his plans with me yet, in case they fall through."

"So, how have you been doing? I see you have the twins with you. I'm assuming that everything went well with the custody case."

The couple that I've never seen before came up behind Jobella. "Eliza, I want you to meet my Mom and Dad, Sadie and Kyle Jordan. They are actually my biological parents. They were missionaries for the last fifteen years, and they were living out of the country. I just met them for the first time during the custody hearing. Kyle was actually Dad's twin brother. They adopted all three of us, so I have my brother and sister back and I couldn't be happier! Oh and guess what! I'm going to have a baby!"

"Oh, I am so happy for you and Steve. That's wonderful! You both deserve this happiness. You do look like your mother with that beautiful red hair you both have. You must have gotten it from her."

Joshua tugged at Jobella's skirt. "Why's she in that wheelchair, 'Bella? Why isn't she moving?"

"She was in a bad car wreck and it hurt her neck. She can't move anything below her neck."

Joanna was next. "Is she gonna' get better?"

"If God wants her to get better, she will." She answered.

"Well, Eliza it was real good to see you again. We need to keep it touch and we still need to have that post wedding party. I promised you guys that."

Billie came up next, after Jobella left. She was still walking with a cane, and had a noticeable limp. Walking beside her was her boyfriend, Danny. "Hi Eliza, sorry I haven't been by to see you. As you can see, I'm still having a little hard time getting around. My therapy is going slow. I'm having a hard time getting back my strength and I'm still in quite a bit of pain. My boyfriend, Danny, has been my rock. We are still planning on getting married in February. I just hope I can walk down the aisle without my cane by that time!"

"I could loan you my wheelchair!" I joked. "Seriously though, I wish for you the best of luck, and good health! I'm glad you have such a great fiancé. Keep in touch with me and let me know what your wedding plans are going to be, okay?"

"I sure will! Maybe you and Jobella can be my bridesmaids."

"What about Zoe, have either of you heard anymore about her?" I asked.

"Not too much. I understand that she is home now, but she has some brain damage. She's like a child in her mentality. They don't know if she'll ever be right again." Billie said.

"That's so sad. I hope she get's better. I will be praying for her as well as you." I said.

Kyle broke into our conversation. "Let me know if you need more help with your foundation. I'm a doctor and I have a ministerial degree as well and Sadie here is a nurse. Just keep us in the loop, okay? There maybe something that we can do."

"That's great! I'll keep that in mind!" I replied, as my parents and I turned to leave. "It was nice meeting you both."

A week had passed, and Eric would be by to pick me up for the candlelight service in a few minutes. I had my mother get me dressed in the prettiest dress I could find and then she did my hair and put makeup on me. My hair had grown out more now and could be styled and I started to look like my old self again. I wanted it to be a truly magical evening with all the candles lit up in the church, and each of us holding our own candle. I guess Eric would have to help me with that.

When the doorbell rang, I didn't want to seem too eager to see him. Mom and Dad met him at the door and since I was in my regular wheelchair for the trip to the church I had to wait on someone to roll me out to greet him anyway.

"Hi beautiful." He smiled when he saw me. "You look gorgeous tonight!"

"You don't look so bad yourself! You clean up pretty good too!" I laughed. I'd never seen him in a suit before.

He rolled me to his car and transferred me to the passenger seat and as he buckled me in he gave me a kiss. "You really do look amazing." He said.

His kiss was magical. It sent shivers down what I had left of my spine. I really did love this man. I prayed that he loved me too.

When we got to the church he put me back into the wheelchair and took me in through the handicapped entrance to the auditorium.

The church was beautiful. There were stained glass windows down the sides of the church, each depicting something about the life of Christ. There was a picture of his birth, his preaching in the temple when he was twelve, one of him turning the water into wine, of gathering the children around him, preaching to his disciples on the hillside, his death on the cross and finally his resurrection. The windows were stunning. I would love to be able to make pictures that beautiful someday.

As we sat in the congregation I was in the aisle way sitting next to him in the pew. He reached over and put his arm around my shoulder. It was such a simple gesture but it told everyone that I was his girl. At least, I hoped that was what he intended.

His parents, brother, and sister came in a few minutes after we arrived and they sat next to him. I didn't think about them coming although I don't know why I thought that they wouldn't. I never met his brother and sister before and I found them to be very pleasant.

I don't know when it happened, but sometime during the service he moved his arm from around my shoulder, and took hold of my hand. After reading the Christmas story and singing a few Christmas songs, we were going to start the candlelight part of the service. It was so pretty as in the darkness one candle was lit, and from that one candle, each person would light the next persons, and so on until everyone in the auditorium had a lit candle. When all the candles were lit, the room glowed. It was symbolic of Christ being the light of the world and each person as they spread the love of Christ, brings a light to the next person until the whole world that was in darkness can see the light of Christ. Eric held my hand around my candle and held his candle in the other hand.

As my candle was lit, I had a strange sensation in my arm. It felt almost like an electrical charge, like I put my hand in an electrical socket. All of a sudden Eric looked at me questioningly. He looked down at my hand, and I followed his eyes to where he was looking. I couldn't believe it. My hand was curling around the candle under his hand and I could feel the warmth of his hand as he held mine.

I looked back into his eyes and saw the surprise registered there. "What just happened?" He whispered.

"I don't know. Maybe it was just an involuntary reflex or something. I don't understand it, but I can feel your hand!"

His dad was sitting next to him and he looked over at us to see what was going on and why we were whispering. He saw that

I was grasping the candle as well. Being a neurologist, he might be able to help explain why I did that, better than we could. We would talk about it later, he said.

After the service was over, we drove back to his parent's house. I was anxious to talk with his father, and he also said he wanted to talk to me. I figured he was going to finally say something about our new business. I was anxious to find out about what we were going to do.

When we got to their house. Eric went around to the back of the car and got my wheelchair out of the trunk and then he did something strange. After he came to open my door he knelt down beside me. I figured he was getting me ready to get out but he didn't make any move to undo my seat belt and I just stared at him. "What are you doing? Are you okay?" I asked.

He just smiled. "I'm better than okay, at least if you tell me what I want to hear. Eliza, I've been in love with you ever since I met you five months ago. Even when you looked more than pathetic, there was something I saw in you and now I want you to be a part of my life... forever. Not just as a business partner, but as my wife. Eliza, will you marry me?"

"Are you sure you want to take care of this messed up body for the long run. It's not going to get any better you know. I love you, but I want everything for you. I can't give you what other women can. You may end up resenting me before it's over. I can be an awful lot of work! I want you to think about the day to day stuff not just the few times we've had together doing the fun things. I can't bring much to a marriage except a bunch of heartaches for you. Are you sure that you know what you're getting in for?"

"My life for the last ten years has been about caring for people who have problems. I wouldn't know how to act any differently. I love you, Eliza. I've loved you ever since we met and I'm not going to get up until you tell me yes. You'd better hurry up, because this gravel is starting to dig into my knees. It's getting cold out here and my parent's are waiting for us."

"You won't regret marrying me, then?"

"Absolutely not! Never in a million years!"

"Well the answer will have to be yes. I love you and obviously, I need you, so the answer is a million times, yes!!!"

He pulled out a box with the most beautiful diamond ring I ever saw and he placed in on my left ring finger.

As he pulled my hand toward him I felt the same electrical charge I felt earlier in the church and I could feel his hand as he put the ring on my finger. It was just as before and I could feel my right hand close around his. Did this mean anything at all, or was it just my imagination, or an involuntary reflex?

His parent's already knew that he was going to propose to me and they were all for it. They thought I would be good for him.

"I'm glad you said yes." his mom said when she noticed the ring on my finger, "Otherwise we would be wasting a perfectly good congratulations cake and ice cream."

"Welcome to the family, Eliza." added his dad when he saw the smile on my face.

They took turns giving me hugs.

After we sat down, his father had an announcement to make to us.

"Son, I want to give you your Christmas present a little early. I wanted Eliza to be here when I gave it to you because it's really for both of you. He went to his desk and he pulled out a file with a ribbon on it. Son, here is a deed to a ten acre plot of land for you to build your rehab and retreat center on."

"Are you serious? That's great! Thanks Dad. You don't know how much that means to us!"

" I do have one stipulation, however."

"Okay," Eric said hesitantly, "do I want to know what that is?"

His father started laughing. "If you're going to have a rehab and retreat center for the physically disabled, you are going to need a medical director. I would like to be a part of your project, Eric. As a neurologist, I think I would be perfect! What do you say?"

" I say, you have yourself a deal, dad!' Eric laughed.

"Is there a building on the lot already, Dr. Evans?" I asked.

"First of all young lady, I'm going to be your father-in-law. So you can call me Ezekiel or Zeke. My patients are the only ones that call me Dr. Evans and no, there is no building on the grounds yet but I think I know just the architect for the job, don't you?"

"I'll have to ask him, but I'm sure he wouldn't mind."

"We'll I wasn't going to say anything, but I've already spoken with your father and he is already putting some plans together for us."

"You are a fast worker! Now I know where Eric gets it from!" I laughed.

"So what would you like to see in a place that that?" His father asked.

Eric spoke up first, since it was his project to start with. I was just here along for the ride.

I would like for it to be a rehab center with a modern day gym and modern equipment. I'd like it to be staffed with occupational, recreational, and physical therapists so that the clients would be exposed to everything that could make their life better, and be more independent. I would like a few nurses that could see to the medical needs of the clients. I'd like a few rooms that could be used as dormitories, so if they didn't have anywhere to go or no one at home to care for them, they could stay there. We could serve as a day care center as well, of sorts for handicapped children, and adults. I'd like to have a small chapel on the grounds somewhere so that we could see to their spiritual needs. Anyone who wants to come there will have to be open to spiritual guidance, so it would be nice to have a chaplain come in if needed, and of course all of our staff should be Christians, or at least be open to working in a Christian facility. I would like to have nature trails with side-walks so that the clients could get around easily, and enjoy the beautiful gardens. It would also be nice if we had a swimming pool where we could work with the patients to help keep them flexible, and it be a fun type of exercise for them."

"Whoa, I'm starting to see dollar signs here, Eric. You have a wonderful vision. It sounds like a terrific idea. I can partially fund your operation, but where will you get the rest of the money to do everything you want to do?"

I plan on doing some fundraising along the way. We want to name our foundation and rehab center for a friend of Eliza's that was in the nursing center with her. We want to call it 'The Akeylia Simmons Rehab and Retreat Center". Akeylia was about the same age as Eliza and had muscular dystro-phy. She wasn't a Christian when they met, and Eliza and her friend Katelyn led her to Christ, and she became a Christian shortly before she died. We thought that this would be a fit-ting memorial for her.

"Her name sounds familiar to me, and so does the name, Katelyn. I remember thinking that they were unusual names. If I remember right, I thought it was unusual for an African-American girl to get muscular dystrophy. It's not something I saw every day."

"Yes, that would be her. So what do you think, do you like that idea?" Eric asked his father.

"I love it! It sounds great! When do you plan on starting the building program?"

"I'd like to start soon, but I know with winter coming up we may not be able to get much accomplished before spring." While we're waiting, we can coordinate our plans, and build an advertising campaign. Plus, there's a little matter of a wedding to prepare for." He smiled at me.

I started smiling then. "You do think of everything don't you? Okay so how do I fit in with all these plans, other than the wedding of course?"

"You're going to be my poster girl, remember?" he laughed. "Actually, I'd like you to be the marketing rep, and business office manager. I've seen you do amazing things with the computer already. We can get you set up with a bunch of hands free, and speech activated equipment, and you'll be able to do anything along that line. You could design all of our promotional materials, and do our ordering, and answer phones. You can do a lot of things."

"You sound like you're going to be a tough boss." I frowned. "I knew you were marrying me for some reason."

"I don't want you to feel too bored. There's an endless list of possibilities for you, if you're willing to do them, of course, or if it suits you better, I can set you up front and lure everyone in with your beautiful face." He laughed. "Or, I can always see if Katelyn would like a job!"

"I get the message, besides, Katelyn is already a part of our plans as well. Between the two of us we can do anything you throw at us." I smiled.

"That's the spirit! You can do whatever you set your mind to. You've survived the last four months. I believe you can handle anything, including me." He replied.

"You got me there."

His mom came into the den bringing cake and ice cream for everyone. Eric stayed by my side to help me eat mine. After we finished eating, we headed for my parent's house.

They were waiting for us at the door when we arrived. Mom was the first to say something. "Well let's see it! We've been waiting all evening for you to come home."

"Oh, you mean this?" I turned my head toward my hand. "Did everyone know about this before I did?"

"It's lovely! Eric you have wonderful taste!" my Mom cried.

"Our little girl is so lucky to have you and we couldn't be prouder of her or you!" said my dad.

"You all act like you knew all about this before I did!" I smiled.

"We did, it was really hard to keep it a secret too. Why do you think I fixed you up so nice tonight?"

"You're dad told me about the land he got for you, Eric. He told me he was going to tell you about it tonight. I hope he did."

"Yes sir, and he said that you agreed to do the blue prints on the buildings. Can you and I get together sometime next week and go over what we want in it?"

"Sure, whenever you're ready." He replied.

After Eric left, I went to my room to get settled down for bed. Mom had tucked me in and kissed my forehead just like she use to do when I was a little girl. "I love you Eliza, and I really like Eric. I'm so happy for you. This is the type of man I always wanted you to have."

Her tucking me in took me back to when I was a little girl and I would dream of my prince charming coming and rescuing me from the evil dragon. Only now it was a real prince named Eric, and the evil dragon was my paralysis. He might not have slain the dragon exactly, but he brought it to its knees.

Chapter 22

I was anxious to contact Katelyn, and let her know about our getting engaged, and about our plans for the new center. The day after Christmas, Eric came by to get me, and he drove us over to the nursing home. I had been home a little over a month now and it seemed strange coming back into the facility. Katelyn met us at the door and we went to her room.

"It's so good to see you again." I said to her. "How is it going?"

"Well I went home for a visit. It didn't go too well, I'm afraid. Mom had Christmas Eve and Christmas off so we got to visit for a little while, but it just wasn't the same as it used to be before I got sick. There were very few presents under the tree, because there wasn't much she could buy for me and obviously I couldn't go shopping for her. She doesn't have a lot of money and I didn't have a way of getting her anything either. We did have a nice dinner though and spent some time together. How about you two?"

"We had a great Christmas. Eric asked me to marry him and we started making plans for our new rehab center. Eric's dad bought a piece of property for us!"

"Oh my gosh, I'm so happy for you two!" She patted my hand and smiled at us.

"Don't forget that you are going to be part of our plans for the center, too," Eric said. "We'd like to put you to work after it is built and would like for you to stay there in the dorm, free and clear, to pay for you working there. That will take a lot of the financial burden off your mother for you having to stay here."

"That sounds awesome, but what could I do?" she asked.

"Eric and I discussed this and he wants you and me to share in doing the marketing and ordering materials and things like that. We both can work using computers."

"We want to be fully staffed with nurse's and therapists and other personnel just like any rehab center. People will be able to stay around the clock that way," Eric added. "As it grows and we get more funds, we'll be able to add other features and other staff. We're going to have some fundraisers and we will have a foundation set up in your friend's name as well."

"I absolutely love the idea. When do you think you'll have it done?"

"Hopefully by the summer, at least the main building, so we can start taking clients, then we'll move into adding on additional buildings. Eliza and I will be building our home on the site as well, so we'll have access to the rest of the facility seven days a week."

"I'm in. I love the idea and I'm so glad you included me on your plans!"

Before we left Katelyn, I asked her if she would like to be one of my bridesmaids at our wedding. "Oh, Eliza, I would love that very much. You and Eric are the best friends I could ever ask for. I'd be beyond excited to do that! Thank you for your wanting me to help out. Between your wedding and helping out with the rehab center, I'll have something to look forward to! You've just made my Christmas a whole lot better! Wait until I tell my mother the plans. She'll be so happy to not have to pay for my care anymore.

Later that day when I returned home, I started to think about my own wedding plans and who I wanted to be with me.

Eric and I decided on a May wedding. We agreed to be married in my family's church. We didn't want to have a real big wedding, just a few close friends, but by the time we thought of everyone we wanted to invite, it got larger and larger. Our folks knew a whole lot of people, especially his parents. They were high society types and didn't want to leave out anyone.

I emailed Jobella and Steve and told them that we were going to get married and I would like her to be my matron on honor if she would. After I sent it, I started thinking that she might not be able to do it because she'd be getting close to her due date by then and I didn't know if she'd be out of school at that time. I would just have to wait and see what she says. Then I contacted Billie as well.

I visualized my wedding as I sent out the e-mails and I started to laugh. If they all accepted, my matron of honor would be waddling down the aisle eight months pregnant, followed by Katelyn in her wheelchair, and then Billie would come hobbling in with her cane, and followed up by dad pushing me in my wheelchair. That should put a few smiles on faces in the audience. Of course Eric and his friends would be all dignified looking, standing there in their tuxedos trying to keep from smiling at my crew. Talk about being poster girls for our new rehab center! We could use our wedding pictures on our website!

Jobella and Billie returned my e-mails and told me they would love to be in my wedding. Jobella said she'd be about seven months along in her pregnancy and she should be fine and Billie said as long as her and Danny were still in the area, she would be happy to, as well. She invited me to her wedding in February, but she didn't say anything about whether I would be in it or not, so I'm assuming she had other plans.

The following week Eric and I went to my father's office to go over the plans he had for our rehab center. He had the whole property laid out in his drawings. He included everything that we had asked for, along with some things we didn't think about. He added a small gift shop and convenience store for the visitors and residents. He laid out the area for the pool and whirlpool spa and the paths through the garden areas. He also put our house plans on it as well. It wasn't too far from the center, but it wasn't too close either. He said we'd need our privacy away from work. He connected each of the buildings with sidewalks so everything was accessible by wheelchair.

We felt excited and comfortable with the plans, and we told my dad that anytime they wanted to, the contractors could get started. We decided together, that we wanted the buildings to be log cabins, giving it rustic look. We wanted to make it feel like a real retreat center. It would be almost like a vacation setting or spa.

Eric's father would co-sign for us to get a loan to get the building program going, but we would be responsible for footing most of the bills that came due later on. We would have to work to get our support base built, and start our campaign fund soon. That would be part of my job.

We had the surveyors and building site inspectors begin their work in February so that come March they could begin the construction.

Eric took me over to our land to show it to me. It was about thirty minutes from Clairmonte. It was a large field and was next to some woods. It was perfect for what we wanted to do.

Next week Eric would be going back to his regular job at the hospital. He had been off for the holidays, but now he had to return to work.

We had three months left to be making plans for our wedding, and in between that and overseeing our building site we would stay busy.

As for me I started making up designs for our center, and started to write pamphlets, and creating business cards and other marketing tools.

I was enjoying the creativity so much, I forgot that I was even paralyzed. My life really was coming together now. I still spent some of the time each evening drawing and painting. I was getting better at it all the time and I finally got where I could paint something worth showing. I started out with flowers and then progressed to still life's and landscapes. Eric and my dad decided to frame some of the pictures and they would hang some of them in the lobby and dorm rooms of our center. They thought that maybe we could put some of them on line or sell them in our new gift shop to help raise money for the center. Of course that gave me the incentive to do more and do them even better. I would love to have classes for our clients that were paralyzed like me later on so they could learn how to do creative things as well.

On Valentines Day, Eric and I went to Billie and Danny's wedding. She looked so pretty as she walked down the aisle with her dad. She leaned against him and when she reached Danny he took her hand, so she was able to go that short distance without her cane. She had a little bit of a limp, but it wasn't as bad as the last time I saw her.

None of the three of us friends were in the wedding party. She actually only had two attendants and they were her sisters. It was a very small wedding with close friends and family.

Danny had just gone into the service and would be getting shipped out in three months after he graduated from college. I hated it for her that they would be separated so soon. I hoped that she would be all right. I know I wouldn't like it at all if Eric were to leave me so soon after the wedding. We all hugged when the wedding was over, and then they had a small reception in the activity building after the service.

That was the last I heard from her for a couple of months, but I knew that she was busy with her new life, and that she wanted to spend as much time with her husband as possible. She wouldn't have much time for her friends right now.

At the beginning of March Mom came into my room one day and said that we really needed to start on our plans for my wedding. It would take a while to pull everything together, especially since everything would have to be ordered. I could look up a lot of things on line and then get with a wedding planner to co-ordinate it. That was the great thing about the Internet you could order just about everything you needed on line and have them ship it to your house. With ordering the decorations, I could just tell the planner and she would gather everything together and make it happen. As far as my wedding dress went, since I'd be in a wheelchair it wasn't that important to have it fit exactly right as long as it was comfortable for me to wear in the chair. My attendants, of course, would have to be fitted. As far as what I wanted for them, I would e-mail them and tell what I wanted and they could go to David's Bridal their selves and choose a dress and get fitted.

I decided that I wanted salmon and teal for my colors. The salmon color because of the beautiful salmon colored roses that Eric got for me when he visited me for the first time in the nursing home after he got his memory back and the teal just because we both loved that color. It reminded me of the ocean and sky on a beautiful summer day, not to mention the fact that the two colors look awesome together.

I told each of my friends that they could choose what ever color they would like the best for their dresses. The bouquets would be the same salmon color roses that Eric gave me.

Eric helped me pick out the invitations we were to send, and Mom did all the mailing of those. How I wish I could help her with it, but obviously I still couldn't do anything with my hands.

I didn't know exactly what I wanted to do about my wedding gown. It wouldn't be easy to find something that would be comfortable in my wheelchair. It couldn't be full because it would be awkward in my wheelchair when I couldn't hold it up. So I opted for a simple A-line dress with a lacy jacket. Mom was going to make a tiara out of teal and salmon color flowers. I would have to settle for a short veil. It ended up being really pretty.

Now all we had to do was wait until everything started to come in. The wedding planner actually came to my house, and helped me to decide what all I had to do and I showed her everything I had picked out. She would have a better idea of everything I needed, and how to arrange it.

While Mom and I and the wedding planner finalized what we wanted, Dad and Eric were in another room deciding on plans for the rehab center and what type of interiors and shelves they wanted.

It was so exciting with all of these plans we were making for our future. I went to bed every night praising God for his goodness. It is so easy to forget him when everything is going so well. We forget that even though we are doing things for his glory, like this rehab center, that we should always give him the thanks for it. If we do it under our own power, it may not go the way he wants it to, and we become boastful of the outcome, if it succeeds, and blame him if it doesn't.

Chapter 23

I was married to Eric in the middle of May. I still couldn't get over the way the Lord blessed me in giving me this wonderful man. He was the love of my life, and had it not been for my paralysis, I would have never met him. Truly all things do work together for those that love the Lord, as it says in the Bible.

We did look a sight coming down the aisle. Jobella was very large for her seventh month of pregnancy. I wondered if she was pregnant with twins, as big as she was. She opted for the teal color dress because it went better with her red hair and she had a hard time finding a salmon color matron of honor dress for pregnant women. My two bridesmaids decided on wearing the salmon color dresses. Billie and Danny were still in town, so she was able to come. She still had to use her cane, however, and she still had her limp. I didn't know if she would ever be normal again. Katelyn came next in her wheelchair. Her mom came to assist her if needed and she pushed her down the aisle and into position. At last it was my turn to come down the aisle. My dad, of course, brought me in. Everyone stood and applauded me as I came in. I wasn't expecting a standing ovation. There was nothing that I had done to deserve that. It was the Lord that brought us together and worked out the details.

I thought that the people would laugh at the sight of us. I'll have to admit we did look comical, but mostly in our eyes. The congregation of attendees was very respectful, and admired us for being able to bring this together with our limitations.

As for me, I was awed that I would be doing this now. I was marrying a wonderful man, so full of potential, and the one who brought out the best qualities that God had given me. He looked so handsome standing there in his teal blue vest and black tux. How I longed to be able to hold him in my arms. Sadly I didn't know if that would ever happen.

In lieu of gifts, we requested that people donate money to our rehab center. Because of that request, at our reception, there was little in the way of regular gifts. Several people gave us cards and money.

After our wedding and reception and saying goodbye to all our friends and family, Eric said he had a surprise for me.

I hadn't been out to our building site since construction started, so I was surprised when Eric drove me there.

"Why are we coming here?" I asked.

"You'll see."

We turned the corner to go down the road to the land. Sitting at one end of it was our home completely built, and ready for us to move in. It was a beautiful log cabin with tall glass windows in the front. It was, of course, a one-story ranch style house with a cathedral ceiling. Eric carried me over the threshold and sat me on the sofa while he went back out to get my wheelchair. While he was gone I looked around at the large living room. I loved the large windows that looked out on the deck and the beautiful trees beyond our house. Because it was spring, the trees were budding out and the dogwoods, azaleas, and forsythia bushes were in full bloom. The windows were facing away from the rehab center and it's construction. Even though we would love our center, we needed to have our privacy and time away from work, as well, so there were no windows on the side of our house facing towards the center. On another wall in the huge room, there was a large stone fireplace with a mantle similar to the one in his parent's home and above the mantle hung my painting that Mom had gotten me with the woman in the wheelchair and Jesus and the angels helping her to stand.

When Eric came back in with my chair, I begged him to let me stay on the sofa for a while longer, but he insisted on showing me the rest of the house. He was so proud of the way it all turned out. He took me first to the kitchen. The kitchen was beautiful and totally equipped to handle someone in a wheelchair. All of the countertops were low enough for someone in a wheelchair to slide under them. *'Too bad I couldn't use my hands and arms to make use of them'*, I thought to myself. I didn't want to hurt his feelings by questioning the rational of making them at that level, if I couldn't use them. Then we went to the bathrooms and bedrooms. The bathrooms had handicap bars next to the toilets and they were tall enough that I could slide over onto it, that is, if I could use my arms to maneuver myself in that way. The bathtub and shower combination was a type of a walk-in, wheelchair accessible tub. Last of all he brought me into the bedroom. He had a specially made king sized bed that had a dual side controls that could be adjusted separately, and could be raised and lowered like a hospital bed.

"Wow…you have thought of everything!" I laughed. "You really are amazing."

"Now let's get out of these uncomfortable clothes, and get relaxed!" He smiled.

As he was helping me off with my wedding dress, he was kissing my neck and shoulders. I felt the shivers down my spine, like I did before, when he kissed me on the night we were engaged. It was a very romantic moment. As he raised my arms to pull the jacket off, I felt the same shocking type feelings in my arms again. As he pulled on the jacket, I jerked my arm back like I was helping him pull it off.

"What just happened?" he asked.

"I don't know. It happened again. It was the same feeling I got on Christmas Eve when I held the candle and you put my ring on my finger."

He proceeded to pull my jacket off my other arm, and it happened again with that arm. Tears came to my eyes. "Do you think that I may be getting feelings back in my arms and hands?" I asked.

"I guess its possible. Your neck was broken low enough that you could regain the use of your arms. You already had feelings in your upper arms and shoulders. I hate to be too optimistic, too soon, after all it's been five months since the last time this happened to you, but maybe we should work on your arms again, just in case it's not a false alarm. You'll need to build up the muscles in your arms again so you can use them and your hands too, if you are getting the use of them again."

After taking my jacket off, he carefully sat me on the bed to take my gown off, and put some comfortable slacks and a tee shirt on me and then put me back in my wheelchair.

He changed his clothes and we went back to the living room and he sat me on the sofa again. I leaned against him and he put his arms around me. I loved feeling so close to him. I prayed that I would get my feelings and movement back in my arms, so I could hold him the way he deserved to be held and I could become more independent.

As we sat there, we opened the cards from our friends and family that we received at the reception. The cards were beautiful and our guests donated close to fifty thousand dollars. His family must have had a lot of wealthy friends. I know my family and I didn't know that many people who could afford to give that kind of money.

Eric and I took the money the next day to the bank to set up an account for the 'Akeylia Simmons Foundation'. He put both of our names on the account so that we both would have access to it and could use it for the center's expenses.

Two days after my wedding I was still having the tingling sensation in my hands and arms. Eric started doing therapy with me to see if we could work on what I was feeling. He did range of motion exercises with me and when he was doing my shoulder rotations, I felt something 'give' in them. The pins and needles feelings stopped and I was afraid that it had reverted back to total numbness again, but when he took my hand to do my elbow movement, I could feel his hand in mine!

"Eric," I cried. "I can feel your hand!"

He took my other hand and it was the same thing. I had feelings in both of my hands again. He took a probe and had me turn my head and tell him when I felt it. I had feelings all the way up my arms. I was ecstatic, but I tried not to get my hopes up too much in case it was another false alarm.

"Now that you have feeling back in you arms lets see if you have the ability to move along with it!" He smiled. "I want to see you squeeze my hand. He held my hand and I squeezed it lightly. I didn't have the strength to squeeze it tight. He changed hands and asked me to do it again. Again, I was able to squeeze that one as well. He was so excited he took me in his arms, and held me so tight I was scarcely able to breathe. When he held me, I felt his hands all the way down to my waist.

I prayed that this wasn't just a fluke. I prayed that coming this close to getting the use of my arms and hands back wasn't temporary, but was real and lasting.

Over the next few days, Eric gave me an extensive workout of my arms. We started out with simple things like active range of motion, and then we tossed a beach ball back and forth and worked with pulleys. All the things he would've done with people in the hospital in physical therapy.

Speaking of physical therapy in the hospital, the day had come when Eric had to go back to work. His vacation days that he took for our wedding were finally over. He hated to leave me alone, but between him, Mom and Dad, and his parents someone was there almost continually to check on me, and of course, he felt better now that I had use of my arms and hands.

After several continuous days of being able to use my arms again, I contacted all my friends and told them the good news. My friends all had news of their own as well. They were all thrilled that I recovered this much, and wished me well on my marriage and on our rehab center. Jobella passed on the news to me that she found out that she and Steve were going to have a little girl, and that the doctor told her they would probably induce labor on her next week. Billie's husband, Danny was being shipped to Afghanistan in a month, after his basic training was finished. He finished college, so he was able to go into the service as a commissioned officer. She was understandably fretful over him leaving so soon. Zoe was at home. Her mother was taking care of her. She was almost like a child in her thinking and doing things. Maybe we could work with her in our facility as well. I told her mom that I would check with my father-in-law about her, to see if we'd be able to work with her at our center.

Katelyn was getting excited about moving into our facility. She was ready to get out of the nursing home, and come and join us. We planned on being open for business in around two months. Eric and I oversaw the rest of the construction. All of the buildings were made of logs, and the main building was two story's high. In the main building we had the reception area, the main rehab gym, and spa area. Off the back of the building we had a temperature-controlled sunroom with a heated pool so that the clients could swim and have aqua therapy year round. On the second story we had ten dorm rooms for the clients that would be living on site. Those would be semi-private rooms so we could hold twenty residents. The clients would be able to come to the gym and ground floor via the elevators. The nurse's station would be upstairs on the same level as the residents.

We had a recreational center that housed a gift shop and convenience store as well as a small cafeteria. It also had a small library that the guests could use.

We had another building that we could use as a conference center and chapel. We would have special speakers and preachers come in on occasion and have at least one church service a week for the residents and any staff that wanted to attend. We would offer the conference center for local groups wanting to use the facility for religious retreats as well.

The rest of the land was divided up into nature areas and gardens and was wheelchair accessible. There would be rest stations for families in each area so they could enjoy the gardens with their loved ones.

Altogether it was a gorgeous place, and I was so proud that Eric was instrumental in getting it built. It was truly a godsend for people like my friends and others with disabilities like me to have a nice place to go to, and be with others with similar problems in an atmosphere of caring and nurturing, a place with godly values and hope.

Epilogue

It has been three years since we opened 'The Akeylia Simmons Rehab and Retreat Center'. Many people have rolled through our doors and became stronger physically and spiritually. Some of them became well enough that they could go out and function in society and even get jobs because of the training in our facility.

Eric's dad, Dr. Ezekiel Evans, is still our medical director and Eric is in charge of the therapy program. Katelyn and I hold the fort down by answering phones, and making sure that staffing needs are met, and we have the supplies we need. Katelyn has blossomed in our program and is my biggest helper. In turn, she now lives at the facility and has all her needs met. She's even attracted the eye of one of our therapists. Occasionally she has times of remission and likes to work in our gardens when she's not at my side helping with all the paperwork. Her mom was able to quit one of her jobs and occasionally helps us out in the store. We took on Steven, Jobella's husband as a part time Christian counselor and pastor until we could hire someone full time. He's been instrumental by God in bringing several people from our facility to the saving grace of Christ.

My dad did such a wonderful job creating the blueprints for our center and overseeing construction, that he has been swamped with projects from people all over this part of the country, wanting him to design their homes and other commercial buildings. In fact he's gotten so much work, that my mom was finally able to quit her job. She occasionally fills in as a nurse when one of our regulars can't come to work.

Eric is in his glory these days. He's loving life even more than ever. Being in charge of the retreat has been a blessing for all of us.

As for me, I'm loving life as well. My arms have stayed healthy and functional since that day after our wedding. I've never gotten the use of my legs back and I know I never will, but praise be to God, I can do anything that he wants me to do. Besides my regular work as administrative assistant and co-owner of the center, I'm painting and drawing pictures that are inspirational in nature and have made some designs for greeting cards that are sold exclusively through our store at the center and on line on our website. Occasionally I still do my artwork using my mouth. People come from miles around to see my latest offerings and all the money from the sales goes right back into our foundation to pay for some of our pet projects. We have some residents and other clients that aren't able to pay, and that's all right. That's why we have the foundation.

But the biggest blessing in my life right now is Eric junior. He'll be two years old this year and he keeps me rolling. If he's not chasing Snickers and Toby around our house, he's getting into other trouble. The clients seem to enjoy his antics when he is in the gym laughing and carrying on, but I'm thankful that his daddy is somewhere close by and has two good legs to chase him down when needed and when he's not there, he makes sure there's at least one other adult somewhere in the vicinity that can control him.

Life doesn't always seem fair at times and we don't always get everything we want or need. Sometimes obstacles get thrown in our way to keep us down and to prevent us from doing God's will, but if we believe enough in his power and are open to anything God wants us to do, he'll provide the means to accomplish it. We can overcome our limitations by taking God's hand. His will is always perfect.

Afterword

Although this is a novel and "The Akeylia Simmons Foundation" and the rehab center in the story are fictitious, there are several handicap foundations and centers that need your help in funding.

I got a lot of my information on what it means to have total paralysis by reading books about real people with disabilities and looking up cases of people on the Internet who are paralyzed, especially from neck injuries and their experiences. That and my experience in nursing, especially with working in a nursing home, helped me to create this story.

One particular organization that moved me especially, was "Joni and Friends". It was founded by Joni Eareckson Tada, who herself is a quadriplegic, and a Christian, and has a ministry of doing amazing things for disabled people around the world. As a result of her willingness to allow me to use her organization in conjunction with this book, I will donate a portion of any royalties I get for this book to her organization and I encourage any of you who read this novel to open your heart and give to your favorite charity that helps people with handicaps.

You can contact Joni and Friends at:
Joni and Friends International Disability Center
(818) 707-5664 or their website:
www.joniandfriends.org

You can also contact me at:
http://www.kardeesangelpublishing.com

Author Bio

Deanna Stalnaker's "Women of God" series began taking shape after she retired from a long career in nursing. It is based on her love of the Bible and what it teaches us for a better life. As a retired nurse many of the references of hospital procedures and nursing care were taken from her years of experience working with patients. Each of the books deals with women going through some kind of medical and/or life dramas and how God had worked in their lives to make them better Christians.

She is currently living in North Carolina, with her husband of 41 years, and her daughter who is also a writer. Her other daughter is married and going to UNC and she has one granddaughter.